Ride to Battle Mountain

RIDE TO
BATTLE MOUNTAIN

LAURAN PAINE

WHEELER
CHIVERS

This Large Print edition is published by Wheeler Publishing, Waterville, Maine, USA, and by BBC Audiobooks Ltd, Bath, England.

Wheeler Publishing is an imprint of Thomson Gale, a part of The Thomson Corporation.

Wheeler is a trademark and used herein under license.

The text of this Large Print edition is unabridged.

Other aspects of the book may vary from the original edition.

Set in 16 pt. Plantin.

LIBRARY OF CONGRESS CATALOGING-IN-PUBLICATION DATA

Paine, Lauran.
  Ride to battle mountain / by Lauran Paine.
    p. cm. — (Wheeler Publishing large print Western)
  ISBN-13: 978-1-59722-580-9 (softcover : alk. paper)
  ISBN-10: 1-59722-580-0 (softcover : alk. paper)
  1. Large type books. I. Title.
PS3566.A34R535 2007
813'.54—dc22   2007016768

BRITISH LIBRARY CATALOGUING-IN-PUBLICATION DATA AVAILABLE

Published in 2007 in the U.S. by arrangement with
Golden West Literary Agency.
Published in 2007 in the U.K. by arrangement with
Golden West Literary Agency.

U.K. Hardcover: 978 1 405 64212 5 (Chivers Large Print)
U.K. Softcover: 978 1 405 64213 2 (Camden Large Print)

Printed in the United States of America on permanent paper
10 9 8 7 6 5 4 3 2 1

BBC
AUDIOBOOKS

2 9 AUG 2008

RIDE TO BATTLE MOUNTAIN

CHAPTER ONE:
ONE CRIPPLED
BUCKBOARD

When wheel-hubs wore, as they invariably did, particularly in a country where the earth was gritty which meant the dust was sharply abrasive all summer long, it was the custom to bush them with two half-round metal inserts, but because most ranch shops and forges were not really equipped to manufacture things out of hard steel, at least no steel that was any harder than horse-shoes, which were largely malleable lead, the inserts might work fine for a short while, but they too, wore through eventually, and the result was more often than not worse than ever. The wheel wobbled dangerously.

If a person was caught out a distance from town or the ranch when one of those inserts let go, there was a fair chance that the wheel would collapse before he got anywhere near a place where some kind of temporary lash-up might get him home.

John Bowman was standing under the

blazing sun swearing with frustration and disgust as he surveyed the slanting rear wheel on the ranch buckboard, fully aware that while he was only about five miles from town, from Shafter where the nearest blacksmith shop was, and was about equally as distant from the home-ranch, over west of Shafter, the lurch and wobble of that wheel with its fragmented insert and worn-out inner boxing, was not going to stand the haul.

If the buckboard hadn't been loaded with salt sacks, equalling probably four hundred pounds, he still would not be able to make it, in all probability, but *with* the rock salt, he did not have a prayer of a chance.

The wheel was one of the original ones that had come with the buckboard, and that buckboard was older by far than John was; his mother had driven it across the prairie from the Missouri River, behind his father's big Conestoga; it had to be at least sixty years old because his parents had not bought it new.

It was early summer, and although the heat did not usually arrive this early, it certainly had this year. In fact John's brother had prophesied a drought year on the range, and that was why he'd sent John over to Wolf's Ferry for the load of salt. He wanted to bait their cattle up into the highlands around Lincoln Lake where there would be good feed until snow fell, probably about late November. Otherwise, keeping the cattle on the home range until the grass was eaten down into the dust, could wipe them out. Also, unless the Bowman B Bar cattle got there first, someone else would pre-empt the upland meadows, and range-law prohibited trespassing upon land already being used and claimed by others.

No one actually owned the range up there. It was a long hard drive to reach the highlands, and anyway, droughts only arrived in Northern New Mexico about every fifteen or twenty years. It wasn't like the desert country lying southward where drought was a way of life and no one every sold *fat* cattle, only *slick* cattle.

A lot more than just the inconvenience of abandoning the wagon and riding the team back to the ranch for help, was at stake. John, at eighteen, was big and rangy, as his father had been and as his brother still was even though his brother was thirty to John's not-yet-twenty, but he was still not as seasoned as an older man would have been, so he stood there feeling helpless and swearing.

He did not see the rider slanting towards the road from the westerly sidehills, partly because the man was behind him and to his left, and partly because John was too sunken in his private misery to look around, or even to care.

But when a shod hoof struck rock he turned, one hand dropping to hover near his hip-holster. Northern New Mexico hadn't been completely tamed yet. For one thing, it was too big; for another, it was too isolated. There were even occasional rumours of bronco bucks rampaging through. John had never seen any. His brother had, but that had been ten years back, about the time the army was mopping up the last of the hostile rancherias.

But it wasn't a mounted Indian. The man had his hat tipped down to brim-shade his bronzed face. He rode easy although he was dusted with light grey from the trail. He looked to be about the age of John's brother, Harlan, but that was something you could never be sure about. In a hot country men seemed not to age so much as they seemed to gradually shrivel with age.

The rider hove to about fifty feet away, leaned upon his saddlehorn with both gloved hands and studied the awry wheel. "Don't look too good," he opined, and smiled.

His horse was thick and powerful, chestnut

in colour and rigged out in the Southwestern style, meaning a centre-fire saddle, rein chains, a silvered bit and doubled Navajo blanket. The man himself wore flat-heeled drover's boots and a stiff-brimmed, low-crowned hat. His gun was tied down and had ivory grips. He looked more to John Bowman like a stage driver or a freighter, than a cowman, but there again, you couldn't ever be sure.

They did not exchange greetings. John simply said. "The damned inserts gave out." He turned back to his study of the buckboard. "Even if I off-load the salt, the rig'll never get me down to Shafter."

The weathered, tanned man shot John a look. "Shafter?"

"Next town. About five miles southward. The smith down there, Abraham Hepler, would cobble up something to get me over home, to the ranch."

The stranger continued to study the wheel a moment before stepping down. He trailed one rein and walked up closer, then squatted to peer under the rig. He slowly turned looking left and right, then his eyes fell upon a large stone as he arose and leaned upon the tailgate. He tapped one of the croakersacks.

"Salt?"

John nodded. "Four hundred pounds of it."

The stranger pointed to the stone. "All right; if you'll set the stone up-ended beneath the axle, I'll fetch in something for leverage, and we'll remove the wheel."

John raised troubled eyes. "What good'll taking the wheel off do, mister? We don't have anything to replace the bushing with."

The stranger smiled. Unsmiling, he looked pleasant, but hard. Smiling, he looked affable and likeable. "We'll figure something out," he said, and turned to step up over leather and rein back around, riding out as he took down his lariat.

For John Bowman, the initiative now rested with the cowboy or whatever he was, and that was agreeable because John surely had no solution. He got the boulder, which was almost as heavy as he was, wrestled it into place beneath the buckboard, and raised up sweating like a studhorse.

The stranger returned dragging a summer-cured, half-dry oak limb. They got it into position atop the rock and beneath the axle, then the stranger lifted the whole rig, load and all, by himself. He had about fifteen feet of leverage so it wasn't as great an accomplishment as it seemed.

John dug out the lug wrench, banged on

it until the nut turned, then he shored up beneath the rig with more rocks, which was hot work, and finally removed the wheel.

They both bent to study the worn old axle. The stranger laughed. "Be nice to have a penny for every mile that axle's covered, wouldn't it?"

John agreed, to be polite; he viewed the worn old axle in a different light. The boxing, too, was worn out-of-round and over-sized.

The stranger said, "What's in the jockey-box," and strolled up to rummage beneath the seat among the old tools, bolts, nuts, scraps of ancient tug-leather, all the odds and ends people had been tossing in there for fifty or more years because they didn't know what else to do with them. He hummed to himself. John waited, positive, now that he had seen the axle and its housing, that there was no way under the blazing sun of mid-morning to reach town with the rig.

The stranger came back with several scraps of the old bone-hard and shrivelled tug-leather. He hunkered in wagon-shade, drew out a razor-honed bootknife, and went to work cutting, measuring, trimming and fitting. When he was finished he had a passable leather bushing which was secured into place by more leather, laid round-wards instead of length-wise. Then he tried to get some hub grease, but there was none, and he shook his head about this, but did not comment. Instead, he hoisted the wheel, worked it gently over the leather bushings so as not to disturb them, then he picked up the wheel-nut and tossed it to John.

"Cinch it down. One thing's in your favour, pardner; the big steel washer that fits beneath the nut won't let the bushing work out." The stranger stood up, and fished out his pocketed buckskin roper's gloves, put them on slowly, watching John Bowman wrench the nut up snug, then he said, "You know, funny thing about cowmen; they lay awake night worrying about grass and water, rain and rustlers, but they never remember to buy a tin of hub-grease when they're in town — and that's what happens. You let steel rub on steel, pardner, and sooner or later it wears out." As John arose, wiping both hands down the outside seam of his trousers, the stranger went over and mounted his horse. "Drive on," he said. "I'll tail you into Shafter. I expect, though, that if you don't try to hurry and get the damned axle hot in there, you'll make it." He lifted his reinhand and laughed as though neither of them had ever had a real problem. "But if you don't make it, why then I reckon we'll have to figure out something else, won't we?"

John clucked up the rested team. As the buckboard moved he twisted to look back. He had misgivings, but the wheel was turning true. Of course, as the stranger had said, five miles was about as long as that makeshift set of inserts was going to hold up. But if the wheel continued to track that long, John would be very pleased.

A mile later, and the wheel still turning straight as a die. John finally grinned at the mounted man riding back there. "I think it's going to work," he said.

The stranger's dark grey eyes showed tough humour. "Looks like it, don't it? By the way, you mentioned a ranch; where you from?"

"B Bar. West of Shafter five miles. My brother Harlan and I run it. Our folks founded the ranch years back. They're both dead now."

The stranger nodded. "B Bar . . ."

"Yeah. Stands for Bowman. I'm John Bowman."

The stranger nodded amiably. He seemed to be one of those naturally amiable, imperturbable, very capable people who perhaps viewed life as all a joke, and could laugh or

15

smile at just about anything.

"Glad to know you, John," he said. "My name is George Lefton."

They drove another mile, then two more miles, and when Shafter finally came into view, trees and rooftops and square-block buildings in a heat-haze rising up off the summer range, George Lefton shed his gloves, tipped back his hat, and began to look expectant, as though he could belly up to a bar and drink a third of his dehydrated weight in beer.

Chapter Two:
An Odd-Looking Stranger

For Harlan Bowman, who had two hired riders with him, the spectacle at the edge of the trees above the hot, drying treeless and brushless southward grazing country, was not just unique, it was downright ridiculous.

The squatting man up there at the edge of the forest was wearing a soiled pearl-grey bowler-hat with rakishly turned and curled edges. It was one of those hats folks saw, in magazine pictures, Eastern financiers and politicians wearing.

Otherwise, the man up there breaking his dry-camp had drover's flat-heeled cowhide boots, trousers stuffed into their heart-tops, faded old levi breeches, a black shell-belt with a tied-down gun — with an ivory handle — and a frock coat of the same elegant pearl-grey colour as the fancy derby hat, and just as soiled as the hat.

Harlan's hired riders grinned. One of them was on the verge of laughing. Maybe the reason he didn't laugh was the same reason Harlan called ahead as the three of them rode slowly up into the shade where the stranger was breaking camp; that ivory-butted sixgun did not look the least bit funny.

The stranger stood up and turned. He had an open, friendly face with blue eyes and thick, shaggy, curly light brown hair. He was lean and sinewy with muscle packed inside a tight, tanned hide. He could have been twenty or thirty years old, and it did not matter a damn.

His horse was mostly thoroughbred, which meant he'd cost someone a lot of money. Not necessarily the thin, supple man wearing the ridiculous frock-coat and bowler-hat, but someone.

The man's rigging was also expensive-looking, the saddle had a half-Mex horn, the bridle had silver, like the bit and the stranger's spurs with their silver-dollar rowels, were also inlaid and overlaid with

17

silver. The man looked plenty capable, but at exactly *what,* neither Harlan nor his pair of riders could guess as they drew rein and the stranger offered the three of them a wide, steady-eyed big smile.

"Boys," he said, "Good morning to you. Now then, if I'm trespassing on someone's range, I'll hustle right up and ride on. I come down out of those inhospitable hills last night when it was darker than the inside of a cow, and made camp the minute I found a place level enough so's I wouldn't roll off in my sleep, so I don't rightly know where I am, or whose land I'm on."

Harlan leaned and studied the man. It was hard not to smile. If Harlan Bowman had ever seen a raffish individual, it had to be this stranger. "B Bar land," he said. "I'm Bowman, Harlan Bowman. My younger brother and I own it. But you're not trespassing; stay as long as you like." Harland finally did smile. "Don't set the forest afire up behind you and don't eat B Bar beef nor ride B Bar horses; those are the only rules. Otherwise, camp here as long as you like."

"Well now," boomed the stranger, raising his right hand for the first time, to tip back his incongruous hat, "that's about as neighbourly a way to meet a feller as I could ask, Mr. Bowman." The stranger's blue-eyed stare showed candid interest as well as appreciation. "My name's Frank Shepherd. Folks been calling me Shep since I was a button down in the mesquite-bean country of Texas — where the wind blows year round, the tumbleweeds roll every autumn, and you can starve to death while you're working your very hardest." Frank Shepherd laughed. He gave an impression of being an extrovert, a kind of booming-voiced clown of a man. Except for that worn, well-cared-for black shellbelt and that ivory-butted six-gun.

"Now then, boys," he said, "could you help me out a little? There's a town around here somewhere, and I think I went and misplaced it."

One of Harlan Bowman's cowboys laughed. "Shafter. Would you know the name of it, Mr. Shepherd? Would it be Shafter?"

Frank Shepherd gazed upon the amused cowboy with a great expression of fondness. "Pardner, that's it. Shafter. Named after some Yankee general, they told me. Now then, I'm obliged to you boys. I'm so obliged that if you'll tell me where this town is, I'll ride on in, clean up a little, and meet you at the bar . . . They got a bar in Shafter, don't they?"

"Southeast about six miles, and there's a bar."

"That's what a town's got to have. Fine. Now then, like I was saying, I'll meet you boys in Shafter in a few hours, and stand the first two rounds at the bar. Old Shep's a man likes to repay favours, believe me, boys."

Harlan Bowman, like his hired hands, could not refrain from being infected by Frank Shepherd's raffish good-nature. "We'll be in this evening," he said. "Can't make it sooner because we're making a gather."

Shep looked at Harlan Bowman. "A gather? Well now, Mr. Bowman, I'm not the best cowman in the world — but ain't it a little early . . . ? Every place I've ever worked cattle they don't gather until a week or such a matter ahead of shipping time."

"Not to ship," explained Harlan, "to drive the cattle into the uplands." Harlan considered Frank Shepherd a moment, as though arriving at some kind of decision about him. Then he waved an arm. "That range is drying up, Mr. Shepherd. In another month there won't be enough grass. There's a big lake and a ring of high meadows up beyond that peak you can barely see behind you to the left — that's Battle Mountain. We figure

20

to summer the cattle up there."

Frank Shepherd listened to all this, then spread his hands. "Well; now you know I'm a stranger to these parts, Mr. Bowman."

That wasn't all Harlan Bowman had just figured out; whatever else Frank Shepherd was, he was *not* a cowman. Maybe he'd been a range-rider like the men sitting their saddles on either side of Harlan, but *they* were not cowmen either, and neither was Frank Shepherd, or he'd have seen from the condition of the curing grass that a drought year was approaching. That was the difference between cow*men* and cow*boys.*

Harlan lifted his reins to turn away. "See you this evening," he said, and spun his horse. The cowboys did the same. They loped out a mile from the foothills then one of the cowboys, a rider named Jim Bates, said, "I can't figure that one out, can you, Harlan?"

Bowman grinned back shaking his head. "Looks like a broken-down faro dealer. Or maybe a preacher down on his luck."

"That feller's no preacher," said the other rangeman, adamantly. "You never saw no preacher wearing his gun like *that.* I got no idea at all what he *is,* but I can sure tell you what he *ain't;* don't cross him."

Harlan's older rider, the one who had

sized up Frank Shepherd on the basis of how he wore his weapon, had ridden for B Bar three summers straight-running. His name was Tim Brophy and he wintered down around Tombstone every year when the riding season was over. He was a good hand; Harlan liked him and Brophy got along well with both Harlan and John Bowman, otherwise, of course, he'd never have returned each springtime to hire on and ride all summer for B Bar. Tim was older than Harlan Bowman by maybe ten years which made him about fifteen years older than Jim Bates. Tim said very little about himself, but two things were obvious; he knew cattle, and he knew men. When he told them now, in an oblique fashion, that Frank Shepherd was not as raffish and frank and clownish as he appeared, Harlan and Jim listened.

But the interlude up along the forest-fringe really was nothing more than something to break the monotony of a day-long sashay to hunt cattle; this was their first duty, and eventually they all but forgot about Frank Shepherd.

B Bar range, having been staked out and pegged down years before most of the other cow outfits had come into the Battle Mountain country, stretched across the heartland of the grasslands stretching east, west, and southward from the looming mountains, which were all overshadowed by one great, grim peak called Battle Mountain. B Bar did not own all the land it controlled, but it owned almost half of it. The rest of it was held by prior right and prior use, things that most cattlemen respected. Not *all* cattlemen, but most.

Harlan, after sending his brother up to Wolf's Ferry before dawn the previous day for the load of salt, had begun his gather the same time John drove out of the yard with the old buckboard. This was the second day. He, with Jim and Tim, had rounded up roughly three hundred cows and bulls, had drifted them close to the home place where they were expected to hang around because the grass was good there, until the rest of the gather had been completed. Altogether, the Bowman brothers ran somewhere in the neighbourhood of six hundred cows and about twenty-five horned bulls. This year, as usual, there were more than a thousand critters because B Bar tried to calve-out in February, which was a little earlier than most stockmen got their calves on the ground in any snow-country, but the father of Harlan and John Bowman had started that practice before his sons were born; it caused him a little extra work — depending upon the weather in February — and he inevitably lost a few calves, but on the other hand, in the fall of the year when he trailed down to the shipping point, he had steer calves weighing anywhere from a hundred to three hundred pounds more than anyone else's steer-end of the calf crop. Mostly, B Bar culled close and kept back the best heifers, which, even when they were bigger and sassier than anyone else's heifers, did not fetch the price per hundredweight that steers brought.

Harlan had grown up with B Bar. He'd been no older than his brother when his mother died, and when, the following year, his father just sat down until he also died, but Harlan was a natural cowman. John was too, but not at eighteen-crowding-nineteen. No one that age is dedicated to anything, unless it's things that don't really make a feller much money or have anything to do with cattle and grass and weight-gains. Like girls and cards and bucking horses, and big heads on Sunday mornings after all-night sessions in barrooms.

Harlan was patient. It hadn't been all that long ago that he'd been just as useless, and he remembered it very well; remembered his father's exasperated look, remembered the head-wags, the mutterings, the grunts of disgust.

He was pointing out a little bunch of cows to Jim and Tim, over in among some creek-willows where the shade and water was pleasant, when he heard someone whoop, and turned to see John coming overland from the direction of town, instead of southeasterly from the direction of the stageroad, and dropped his arm. "You boys pick up those critters," he said, "and drift them on to the ranch. I'll go see why in hell John went all the way to town with that salt, instead of cutting inland."

Tim, eyeing the oncoming buckboard, smiled a little. "Just remember," he told Harlan, "you were eighteen once." Then Tim jerked his head and led off at a lope with Jim Bates following along.

Harlan looped his reins, stepped down and stood in the shade of his horse, waiting. When John came close enough Harlan pushed back his hat and looked past to the rear of the wagon. The salt was there.

John halted his team and said, "Damned near didn't make it," and jerked a thumb towards the nearside wheel. "The insert gave out five miles up the road. Some stranger came along; between us we got the wheel off and he made a bushing out of old tug-leather that got me to Abe's shop in town. I been there over an hour while Abe made another insert. Harlan; why don't we just retire this old buckboard and get us a new one?"

Harlon strolled over and gazed thoughtfully at the rear wheel. "Did you pay Abe?" he asked.

"Two dollars," replied John, stepping down to walk back in the heat. "That's more than the buckboard is worth."

Harlan did not argue this point, but he said, "Just because a wheel or an axle or a bushing gives out, John, is not any reason to buy a whole new wagon. You'd better learn that the best way to have money is to save it when you get it. Who was the stranger?"

John looked disgustedly at the repaired boxing. "I don't know. He said his name was George Lefton. He sure saved my bacon. If he hadn't come along I'd have been sitting out there yet."

"Cowboy?" asked Harlan, turning back towards his horse.

John stepped up into the buckboard and leaned for the lines as he replied. "I don't know what he was, Harlan. Looked more like a freighter to me, or a stage-driver. All I know is that he sure was handy with his hands, and had ivory grips on his sixgun."

Harlan mounted, evened up his reins and

looked at his brother. "Ivory handles?" He was thinking back to the early morning when he had also met a stranger with ivory butts on his sixgun.

John said, "Yup," clucked up his team, turned the buckboard and headed for the home place to off-load the salt sacks.

CHAPTER THREE:
RENDEZVOUS

The town of Shafter had indeed been named for an army officer, General John K. Shafter, who had served well and doggedly, if not altogether outstandingly, in the War Between the States, but exactly *why* the town had been named for General Shafter no one seemed to know. Maybe, some said, it was because, many years back, the town had been an outpost, a frontier fort. But the fallacy there was that old General Shafter never served in New Mexico. Well, it didn't really matter; a town had to have some kind of a name and Shafter sure beat some of those Mex names the towns down south along the border, and inland throughout the desert country, had.

There was a town down there called Guadalupe, which wasn't too bad, as Abe Hepler was explaining to the stocky stranger who'd ridden in to have his bay horse re-shod, but as a matter of fact the full name of the town, in Mex, was something like Village Of The Blood Of Our Sacred Lady Of Guadalupe. By comparison, naming a town Shafter for a general who had never even been near Shafter, New Mexico, wasn't so crazy, was it?

The stocky man laughed. "Not crazy at all," he said, leaning in hot shade gazing up the tree-shaded wide roadway. "And it's a right pleasant town to look at. Not too many cowtowns have trees, and glass windows among the store-fronts."

Abe, who was a huge, massive, darkly bearded man, put down the horse's foot, stepped to the doorway and aimed with his nailing-hammer. "How many got brick buildings? See that fine brick building yonder next to the Oxbow Saloon? That's the First National Bank of Shafter. Not even too many cowtowns have banks."

Abe went back into the hot, stifling gloom of his shop to continue working.

The stranger was a thick-necked, heavy-shouldered man with perpetually narrowed eyes as though he had spent all his life upon the desert. He had travel-stain on him, and his flat-crowned hat had sweat stains half way upwards from the brow-band. He stood slackly making a cigarette with white paper, which was unusual in a wheatstraw, brown-paper-cigarette country, and looked completely pleasant and relaxed.

When he was ready to light up, he scraped the match with his right hand upon the warped and roughened old siding directly beside him, a few inches above the tied-down six-gun in its russet holster; six inches above the graceful ivory handle of his six-gun.

The town was drowsing. There were a few people, mostly bonneted women, on the plankwalks, doing their shopping probably, and there were some sleeping horses, saddled and standing hipshot, up in front of the Oxbow Saloon — which also had a card room out back — but otherwise the town of Shafter was dozing away another summer day. It was a trifle early for really mid-summer weather, the blacksmith had told the stranger, as he'd sized up the handsome, young, bay horse before leading it inside to start work, but if there was one thing a man couldn't set any real store by, it had to be the weather.

The burly man had smiled total agreement. Now, he leaned there, smoking, studying the brick building up yonder next door to the saloon, and when a horseman appeared far northward approaching town at an easy walk, the burly man's gaze narrowed a little, then it widened when the oncoming stranger was near enough to be recognised. There was an old buckboard ahead of the horseman, moving slowly, it looked to be loaded with something. The burly man dropped his smoke, ground it out under a flat heel, then waited until he was sure the buckboard would turn in at the smithy, before drifting over across the roadway to lean in the overhang shade outside of the general store.

The horseman who had accompanied the buckboard dismounted from a handsome chestnut gelding, waved off the lad's thanks in the buckboard, and with no more than one long, casual glance at the burly man leaning in the shade out front of the general store, led his mount down to the liverybarn and left it there.

On his way back, the burly man with the ivory-handled sixgun was still across the road, so the other man angled across, casually. When they were close the burly man grinned. "Made it did you, George?" he said, and the other man, taller, not as wide nor powerful, smiled back.

"Sure. I expected to, Hank. Any sign of Shep yet?"

"Nope. But you know Shep; he could get side-tracked almost anywhere there was a pretty widow-woman, a dice game, or maybe a little horse-trading that needed doing." The man named Hank looked across the road. "Where'd you pick up the kid and the old buckboard?"

"About five miles north up the roadway. We cobbled up a bushing for his near-side rear wheel and limped him on into town." George Lefton straightened a little and looked up the roadway. "Nice town. Peaceful, quiet; how long have you been here, Hank?"

"Not long, couple of hours. The smith over there is putting on a new set of shoes for me."

George frowned faintly. "I thought you had a new set put on just before we — got active — up in Laramie."

"I did, but have you got any idea how far Laramie, Wyoming is, from Shafter, New Mexico?"

George smiled without humour. "Where do you think I came from — heaven? The shoes on my horse aren't worn out yet."

"Then you'd better take another look," muttered Hank, and twisted to glance indifferently up the roadway. He stiffened. "My gawd; will you look up there?"

31

George looked. "Where in hell did he get that hat and that pearl-grey coat?"

"The damned idiot will attract attention in a place like this," growled Hank, and swore a little. "You know, sometimes I wonder about Shep."

Frank Shepherd did not ride down as far as the blacksmith shop, but he obviously had seen, and recognised, the two men standing under the overhang out front of the general store because, as he turned in by the saloon hitchrack, he raised one arm in a big casual salute, then he stepped down, looped his reins, and without another glance, barged through the batwing doors and disappeared from sight.

Hank straightened up and heaved an audible sigh, but George quietly laughed. "Don't stew so damned much," he told the burly man. "No one down here even sees a newspaper until it's a year old. Shep wants to come into Shafter looking like something the cat dragged in, what harm can it do?"

"Plenty," stated Hank. "The idea is to look like you belong with the scenery, not like you're a cross between a holy-roller preacher and a skunk-trapper. George, for your information, a year old newspaper is a lot more dangerous than a brand fresh one. By now we're no longer news up in Laramie, but we *were* news a month back, and *that* kind of a newspaper can get us all hanged real easy." Hank's indignation seemed to increase rather than diminish. "Why in hell do you figure we went to all this trouble, heading for this gawd-forgotten cow-country by three separate routes? Not so's that damned idiot at the bar, up yonder, can draw attention to us, and that is a bald-faced fact."

George remained placating. "Hank . . . All right, he didn't have to arrive like that. But I haven't seen anything like a town, let alone a city, since I got below Denver and easterly a hundred miles, so don't worry. Like you said up in Wyoming; there are no telegraph lines down here, and even the stages only run when they feel like it. No one is going to make any connection between us and Laramie, a month ago. Now let's go up and have a drink. And *don't* start eating Shep out. Understand?"

Hank looked across the roadway where Abe Hepler was now working on the salt-laden buckboard, which meant he'd be another hour, at the very least, getting back to shoeing Hank's horse. The idea of a drink was a good one, so Hank turned and trudged along northward past the cafe, past the land office, past the combination doctor-undertaker's little gloomy building, and on up to the saloon. There, Hank stopped and stared.

"Now where in the hell did he get that big thoroughbred horse?"

George answered cheerfully. "Stole it, probably. Come along."

"Wait! If that idiot went and stole a horse *too* . . . Do you remember what we agreed on up in Wyoming? After we finished in Laramie, we wouldn't turn a single hair on anyone's head until we met down here in this backwater town, because we didn't want to leave any trails?"

George looked impatient. "I remember. Now let's go get something cold . . . And if you're wise, you won't start out making an issue about that horse. For all we know, Hank, he bought it."

Hank rolled his eyes and snorted, but he did not speak his mind, which was probably just as well.

They entered the Oxbow Saloon side by side. The room was not exceptionally deep, but it was long; in fact it looked as though someone had bought two shops and had knocked out a partition to make the room that long. The bar was something very rare west of Chicago and east of San Francisco — it was carved mahogany.

The entire interior of the Oxbow Saloon belied its frontier range-country name. There was a back room where the poker tables were covered with split rawhide, then varnished, and there was a carpet on the floor back there.

Over the bar was a handsome picture of a woman with most of her clothes on. She was a bosomy woman, but mostly, she had a very beautiful face; it had a dark, hauntingly sensitive look. No one had painted that picture just to be painting a beautiful woman. She had *lived,* somewhere, some time.

The barman who was serving Shep was a gross, thick, black-eyed man with a great, upcurling black moustache. He looked completely different from the exquisite woman above him in the elegant, carved frame — or did he? As George strolled up on one side of Shep, and as Hank strolled up on the other side, George thought he saw something elusive, but nonetheless *there,* that hinted at some connection between the thick, gross man, and the exquisite, sensitive woman.

Shep turned and beamed. "George, you're a sight for sore eyes, by gawd you really are. And Hank, you are too. I never was right sure we'd ever —"

"Where did you get that damned thoroughbred horse tied up outside?" hissed Hank, watching the barman down a ways drawing off two more sudsy beers.

Shep considered the burly Hank a moment with an expression of mingled outrage and hurt. Then he said, "The same place I got me this here swallow-tail coat and this here curly-brimmed beaver-belly hat. Did you ever see the quality of a hat like this before, Hank? No, you never did, because you didn't never mingle with the kind of folks —"

"You stole the horse," hissed Hank, "didn't you?"

Shep looked down his nose. "I won that horse, and this hat, and this hammer-claw coat, from a fake of a preacher up in Denver. Well; below Denver at a place they just renamed Colorado Springs. I met him in a place run by a woman named Maisie, a sort of cardhouse and —"

"Never mind," said Hank quickly, as the bartender returned. Hank dropped a coin atop the bar, waited until the barman departed, then reached for his beer.

Shep went on where he'd been interrupted. "I met this here old hypocrite who was bible-banging all the cowtowns and making a killing at it. We got into a little game of poker with couple other fellers, cowmen I think they was, and I concentrated on that damned fake preacher. I won his hat. Then I got this here claw-hammer coat. Then the others dropped out and we drew — best hand — and I took his thoroughbred horse." Shep smiled fondly in recollection. "He'd have shot me. He wanted to. He stuck his right fingers inside his vest where he had a little belly-gun hid out. But you know, a preacher can't shoot folks, and all them cowmen was standing around. But I didn't waste much time switching my outfit to the thoroughbred horse and getting the hell out of there. Now then, Hank Burton, you sour-faced, bull-built suspicious old billy goat, aren't you ashamed of yourself?"

Hank did not say whether he was ashamed of himself or not. He simply drank down that first beer and signalled for the beefy, unsmiling, black-eyed barman to come get his glass and refill it. Then he leaned upon the bar and sighed.

"It's been one hell of a long ride," he murmured.

Shep was too busy draining his glass to reply and George was leaning down, his glass still two-thirds full, gazing up at the hauntingly beautiful woman over the backbar, too engrossed to even hear what Hank said.

CHAPTER FOUR:
THE FIRST DAY IN SHAFTER

Hank got a room at the hotel, which was upstairs over Pardee's gunshop, and turned in early. George Lefton went down to the cafe and had a steak with potatoes, apple pie and coffee. Then he and the cafeman, a slovenly individual who had cowboyed for twenty-five years until a bad fall had broken both his legs and had left him a little stiff and achey, sat and smoked two cigars — which George had brought down from the saloon — and talked. It was eight o'clock by then, anyone who'd been in for supper had come and gone long ago.

Shep, because he had his rendezvous with the B Bar outfit, was still loafing up there at the Oxbow Saloon, and although the gross, sour-faced black-eyed bartender never smiled and only grunted when Shep gave him an order, it was obvious that as long as Shep spent money in his saloon the disagreeable barman would restrain what appeared to be his dislike of a man like Shep, who joked a lot, and was a little noisy, and was dressed in that ridiculous bowler-hat,

38

and that undertaker's coat.

For George Lefton, it had been an ideal day. When he'd left Laramie, up in Wyoming, he knew, as well as his partners also knew, what they had to do next. They knew how to do it as well. But for a long time George had ridden through mountains and forests and had skirted around plains and prairies so as not to be seen, on his way down to New Mexico, and he wondered if he would ever see Hank and Shep again — or if they would ever see him again.

A man does a lot of thinking, riding a lonely, long trail. By the time George Lefton found the town of Shafter, he'd made some decisions. Eventually, he proposed telling Hank and Shep, but right now he was content to smoke his cigar, drink a little coffee with the overweight cafeman who wore slippers instead of shoes or boots, and just talk about casual things.

The cafeman's name was Charley Santee and although he had been in the Battle Mountain country for ten years, he told George he had been born in Indian Territory and had mostly worked the Southwest, which was actually where George and Hank and Shep had been born and raised, and had met, working for the Gun Creek Cattle Company in central Arizona. It had been on a three-man gather for the Gun Creek outfit that George, Hank and Shep, hunkering around their cooking-fire one night over a year back, had discussed the elemental affair of making a living, and had come up with a not-very-remarkable discovery: A man could make it slow, working cattle and saving his money, or he could make it fast, *not* working cattle and taking the money other people had saved.

Three months later the trio rode into Laramie at the tag-end of shipping season. They had planned for a month, then had scouted the north country for another month, and the third month they had struck, three men with ivory-handled six-shooters, and had disappeared on the wind.

George had repeatedly told his partners that his ideas about outlawry centred around doing exactly what they had done; pick a bulging bank, be absolutely certain how much money was in that bank, then plan the robbery so perfectly that it would go off like clock-work — which it had — then disappear and never rob another bank, no matter what.

The three of them had mulled that over hour after hour, down in central Arizona, on the trail northwards towards Wyoming, and for a few weeks before they struck.

George's idea was elemental; if no one knew you, if you had no record as an outlaw, and if you made your strike fast then dropped from sight, an awful lot of people would hunt you, no doubt about that, but they wouldn't be hunting any particular trio of outlaws, they would simply be hunting three unknown men, and the chances of them ever finding you were about nine-to-one.

That is exactly how it had worked out, so, as George sat slouched over the counter in the cafe listening to the cafeman's rambling dissertation about the Battle Mountain Country, he was completely relaxed and comfortable. He was confident that they would never be found, providing none of them ever confessed, drunk or sober, and providing none of them ever again went outside the law to tempt the fates.

The cafeman recollected the time a couple of men had tried to rob the brick bank up the roadway. That had occurred six or seven years back, Charley Santee was not sure which, but then Charley Santee was always hazy about dates. He knew *seasons;* it was hot or it was cold, but like many rangemen, he had never in his life paid much attention to days or weeks, months or even years. In this respect rangemen were a lot like the Indians they had replaced.

George was interested in the robbery. "How much did they get?"

Charley Santee's pale, round face creased into a grin. "Nothin'. Well; that ain't exactly right, either. One of 'em got a load of quail-shot in the back as he run for his horse, that near cut him in two, and the other one got his horse killed under him on the edge of town. Abe Hepler the blacksmith, done that. They brought him back and locked him in the jailhouse up next to the bank. We didn't have a full-time lawman then. We still don't; Abe doubles for that when it's needed. That same night, after Abe had went home to bed, they took him out and hanged him to the tree growing in front of the bank. The tree's still there." Charley Santee grinned at George. "Someone said it was poetic justice. I'm not right clear on what poetic justice is, but I can tell you one thing, they sure hung him right where he deserved to be hung."

Charley refilled their cups and hoisted his bulk back upon the stool behind his counter. Then he savoured the cigar a moment before speaking again. "There was only one real complaint about that lynching. Dorry Sloan didn't like it at all."

George said, "Who's he?" and Charley Santee's little pale eyes blinked.

"He? Dorry Sloan ain't a he, she's a she. That's right, I keep forgettin', you're new around here. Well, I'll tell you, pardner: Dorry Sloan's just about the most handsome woman you ever seen in all your life. Now wait a minute; I know, you seen a lot of heifers, but don't go contradicting me until you've seen her." Charley Santee pulled on his cigar, trickled smoke, then his face brightened. "Say; by any chance you been up to the saloon?"

George had. "Yeah. A while back."

"Well; did you see the painting of that lady over the backbar?"

George removed his cigar. "That's Dorry Sloan?"

Santee's little pale eyes glowed. "Oh; you *did* notice the picture, did you?" Santee laughed at George Lefton's expression. "Well now, pardner, is she or ain't she?"

George didn't answer. "She's alive?"

Santee's eyes widened. "Alive? Why of course she's alive. She's got that dress and dry goods store at the north end of town. Did you happen to notice that burly, dark-looking devil who runs the saloon? That's her brother, Herb Sloan. Mean bastard. Well; if you get drunk and troublesome in his place Herb's mean. Otherwise he's just surly." Santee thought that was funny and laughed.

George remembered the painting very well. "Is her name really Dorry?"

"Dorothea," explained Charley Santee. "But that's pretty much of a mouthful so folks call her Dorry. She come to Shafter about eight years ago, with Herb. They come from somewhere back east, and Herb brought that fancy bar of his in two wagons. You know, when he set up shop, most of us was half afraid to go in there, it was so fancy. Well; that's what his bar was like back in St. Louis, he told us, and that's the way it was going to be out here in New Mexico. I figure Shafter's got the most elegant saloon this side of the Missouri River."

George Lefton smoked and hunched over the empty counter, and sipped his coffee. "Dorothea. That's a pretty name, isn't it?" He looked over at Charley Santee. "She's not married?"

"Nope."

"That's hard to understand."

Charley said, "Nope," again. "Not around here. Who would a woman like that marry; some horsesweat-rangerider; some dung-booted cowman? Nope. But there's been plenty of them get a big bow in their necks and strut around her. I'd say they've all had a try at it. 'Specially come springtime, rutting season you know; they commence all over again. Once, when I took a herd of Matador cattle up to Forth Worth, I seen some peacocks in the city park. Did you ever see any peacocks?"

George hadn't. "No."

"Well; they're sort of extra fancy chickens. Anyway, I watched them peacocks. They strutted and preened and faunched around the hens in their finest feathers, all slicked up and proud-like." Charley giggled. "That's what it's like round town here come springtime, especially when the new riders drift in for work. You know, I'll bet Dorry's sold more fancy bolt-goods to fellers who'd later chuck the cloth under a tree somewhere, than you can shake a stick at."

George was interested. "Maybe she just doesn't like men."

Charley shrugged thick, sloping shoulders. "Maybe. Only her and me have been friends for years. I don't think it's that, I just figure the right man ain't come along. I also figure, in a place like this, he ain't never going to come along, either. Maybe up in Denver or down around Deming or over in Texas somewhere, in one of them big towns she'd find him, but not around the Battle Mountain Country."

Charley was finished with this subject,

which he had evidently discussed many times before. He said, "Did you ever hear how that mountain up there got its name of Battle Mountain?"

George hadn't, and what's more he really didn't much care. Every place he'd been had a place called Battle Mountain, Scalp Creek, Adobe Walls, Washita or something like that, all of them commemorating some locally famous fight, usually between redskins and soldiers.

"Well, sir," said Charley, willing to take off on this tangent with more enthusiasm than he'd displayed on the Dorry Sloan subject, "Before I settled around here, in fact about ten years before, a band of 'paches had a rancheria up there, from which they used to terrorise the countryside for a hundred miles in all directions . . ."

George sipped coffee, smoked his cigar, and thought of the hauntingly beautiful picture over the backbar, while Charley Santee went on with his lengthy and detailed story of how the army had attacked the Apache rancheria one late autumn when most of the bucks were on a big foray down into Mexico, and had wiped out the entire band at the rancheria, then had set up an ambush, and when the plunder-laden broncos had returned, bringing with them almost two hundred stolen horses with Mex brands, the army had pitched into them and wiped them out too, right near the base of Battle Mountain.

Charley had made quite a study of that fight; in fact he was the local authority about it, probably as much because most of the cowmen, whose fathers and uncles had managed to come away with most of those Mex horses plus other plunder, never talked much about it, as because Charley, who had fought a few Indians in his time, was interested in scrapes of that kind.

He even had some old weapons from the battleground which he offered to show George Lefton, as well as a box full of Indian junk he'd traded for over the years that had come from the rancheria. But George had finished his cigar, had finished his coffee, and was ready to call it a day, so, as he arose, thanking Charley Santee for the extra coffee, he said he'd like to see those things some other time, and walked out of the cafe.

The night was warm, the stars were as clear and brilliant as polished crystal, the town had a few lights up its main stem, and there was evidently quite a party in progress up at the Oxbow Saloon, where Shep and the B Bar men were whooping it up.

But George cut across the roadway heading for the liverybarn to look in on his horse. He wasn't a really good drinking man anyway. Neither was Hank Burton, but Frank Shepherd was. Shep could out-drink most men; George had seen him do it upon a number of occasions. He never worried about Shep like Hank did, but then Hank was a chronic worrier. He was probably up there in his bed at the hotel right now, having nightmare-visions of a big posse boiling down out of the northward mountains.

George grinned to himself and entered the weakly lighted liverybarn, saw the snoring nightman asleep on some horse-blankets in the harness-room, and went quietly down the row of stalls looking in at all the horses, his included. They had all been fed and watered and cuffed down, and even the ones that looked owlishly back at George, were full as ticks and content.

Chapter Five:
Two Fast Shots

Harlan Bowman finished his gather on Tuesday and loped into town to pick up an extra hand or two, now that he was ready to make the drive up to Lincoln Lake near Battle Mountain. He had Frank Shepherd in mind, not particularly because he was convinced that Shep would be a tophand, he still had doubts about that, but because after that wild night at the Oxbow, Harlan knew enough about Shep to know he was tough and resourceful, shrugged off discomfort and inconvenience; in short, Harlan Bowman had sized Shep up to be a good man on the trail, which was a good judgement. Shep had never known anything but hardship all his life; he knew how to laugh in the midst of a drenching downpour, or to make jokes when his throat was parched from heat and thirst. His kind made the best range-riders.

But Shep was not in town when Bowman arrived. As Hank noted to George Lefton down in front of the liverybarn, now that Shep had discarded that ridiculous bowler-hat and swallow-tailed coat, and had settled into the community as the boon companion of the cowmen and cowboys, he was rarely in town any more, which was perfectly all right with Hank — sort of.

"He's so damned rough and ready," complained Hank. "He drinks with 'em, rides with 'em, and sooner or later someone is going to commence wondering just how he manages so well, without ever working. There never was any such thing as a rich cowboy, and everyone knows that."

George smiled. "Did anyone ever tell you, Hank, that for a man, you worry more than an old granny?"

Hank turned with a scowl. "Listen George; with fifty thousand dollars each, we *all* ought to worry a little."

A tall, tanned cowman strolled over and nodded, breaking up the private conversation. "My name's Bowman," he said. "I heard up at the saloon you boys might know where I could find Frank Shepherd."

Hank stiffened, eyeing Harlan Bowman. George felt this rather than saw it. "All we can tell you," replied George, "is that he's not in town. I think he went to help some outfit make a gather over east of town somewhere."

Bowman's interest quickened. "Make a gather? Who would be doing that, I wonder?"

George had no idea. "If anything was said about who it was, Mr. Bowman, I wasn't paying much attention."

Bowman's eyes narrowed a little. "Too early for trailing out," he murmured, more to himself than to the others, "so that'll mean someone is going to the mountains." He turned on his heel and walked briskly back up towards the saloon. Hank, who eyed Bowman's departure, suddenly said, "Hell; if he had in mind hiring Shep on . . ." Hank paused, still eyeing Bowman, who was almost up to the saloon by now.

George guessed his friend's thoughts. "Go after him, Hank. Shep wouldn't take a steady job anyway. Maybe this is what you need; find out if he needs an extra hand and hire on with him."

Hank's entire demeanour altered. This was something he understood; being a rich outlaw was too new, too fretful, he hadn't got used to it yet, and perhaps he never would get used to it, but cowboying was something he knew well and had done all his mature life. "Yeah," he said, and smiled at George, the first such expression he'd shown since the bank robbery up north. "Yeah, I think I'll do that."

After Hank had walked briskly in the direction of the saloon, George ambled over to the tonsorial parlour, got a shave, a haircut, and a bath in the shed out back, then, smelling wonderfully of French toilet water, he too ambled northward up the plankwalk through tree-shade, passing a number of people he and his pardners had come to know, at least by sight, and when he passed the saloon he did not even look over the top of the batwing doors.

Beyond the saloon was the brick bank building. Next to the bank was the rarely-used jailhouse, also of brick, with one side made of stone and mortar. Beyond the jail-house was the dress shop.

He had no excuse for going in there, so he teetered on the plankwalk out front, rocking up and down with his back to the glass window, gazing over across the road-way where four boys in their early teens had a mustang in an old pole corral. The boys were almost as afraid of the little mustang as he was of them. It was a Mexican stand-off, the little, ugly, big-headed shaggy horse in his corner, glaring and softly snorting, the boys in their corner, whispering their strategy. George smiled; he'd been there, many years back, and based upon his own experience, he did not believe those boys would ever get up their nerve to try and rope the little wild horse, let alone saddle and bridle, and ride him.

He was wrong. One boy, tow-headed, wearing knee-breeches and high, coarse grey stockings, came out of the huddle with a lariat. George watched with interest. The little horse rolled his eyes and ducked his head a few times. The lad made his cast, and, miracle of miracles, the noose settled with unexcelled precision right over the horse's head, but the second the horse hauled back and felt the noose tightening, all hell broke loose, exactly as anyone who knew mustangs could have predicted.

George left his position in front of the dress shop to go watch from outside the old corral. He was half-way across the road when the mustang made a charge, scattering the other three would-be horsebreakers. They flew over the rotting old corral poles, yelling, but the fourth lad, the one who had made the accidental catch, clung doggedly to his lariat. That slowed the horse just enough to allow the other lads to escape, but moments later, when the wild horse lunged to leap over the corral stringers, two of which were so old and rotten that they broke under his weight, the lad at the other end of the rope went down in the dust. He was being dragged to a certain violent collision with a corral post.

George ran, and as he did so he yelled to the boy. "Let go the damned rope!"

The boy did not answer. He was being dragged across through the spiralling dun dust, one arm fully extended. The mustang cleared the corral, paused one second because he was facing George, then he turned, dug in hard, and went blindly charging towards the open range beyond town.

The boy yelled something, but dirt and dust choked it off as his body flew over the two punky corral stringers. George heard him hit, heard him cry out, saw that the lariat was caught round a big button on his jacket-sleeve, and as George lunged desperately to grab the rope as it whipped past, he missed and the boy struck down hard outside the corral, limp this time, and no longer resisting. The other three lads were crying out for help.

George hauled up short, drew and fired twice. It was an automatic response with him. The wild horse, suddenly freed of his dead-weight burden, dug in harder and raced like the wind, the broken lariat snapping and curling in his wake.

George holstered his gun, turned back shakily and knelt to turn the unconscious boy over onto his back. He was bleeding from the nose and had a cut up from the top of his forehead into his hair, which was also bleeding.

George freed the lariat from the lad, eased his arm down, then turned. The other three boys were staring at George in stony silence. He said, "What's his name?"

"Carl Hepler," one lad replied weakly. "Mister — is he dead?"

George did not answer the question. "One

of you go get his paw, another of you go get the sawbones. And you there, in the blue shirt, you go fetch me a bucket of clean water; and *run,* the lot of you!"

He turned back with hot sunlight on his back. The boy groaned a little. George moved so that his kneeling, thick body provided shade. He only looked up when someone said, "Good Lord!"

He looked up and recognised her from the picture over her brother's backbar. Only now she was so pale her dark eyes looked enormous. She said, "Is he — shot?"

George blinked. "Shot? No; he roped a wild horse and got hung up in the lariat."

"But I heard two gunshots over here and saw the children running."

George did not explain. The boy groaned again, more strongly this time, and opened his eyes. They rolled aimlessly for a moment, then settled upon the beautiful woman. He moistened his dust-caked lips and tried to smile. "Howdy, Miz Sloan."

The woman knelt, used a lace handkerchief that was scented to wipe away most of the blood and dirt, then she said, "Where are you hurt, Carl?"

The lad was being brave. "Everywhere," he muttered, and rolled his gaze round to George. "Mister — what happened?"

George sighed. He was perspiring under his shirt and across his forehead. "You got dragged," he told the lad. "And the next time you try something like that, don't do it in a corral that's already half fallen down. And don't do it unless you've got a man around. That was foolish; just plain foolish."

The boy winced and the beautiful woman's head came up quickly. She glared. "He's hurt; that's no way to talk to him when he's hurt."

George nodded grimly. "Lady, if that kid was mine he'd hurt a whole lot worse and in a different place before he got to the supper table tonight."

The blacksmith came running up, worry making his big bearded face twisted and ugly. He sank to both knees just as the shock wore off and pain started. The boy whimpered. "I'm hurt, paw, I'm hurt."

Others came up. One of them a wispy, thin man with very little hair atop a smooth scalp. This man, older than the others, took command at once. "Lift him," he told the big blacksmith. "Easy now, Abe. Fine. Pack him over to my office."

The crowd moved away with the blacksmith and the older man, leaving George with the beautiful woman, Dorry Sloan, and two of the lads who had been involved with the wild horse. They stood soberly to one side eyeing George without showing any expression and without speaking. He was not conscious of them as he watched everyone trooping across the road towards the combination doctor's and undertaker's office. Finally, he dusted his hands and said, "He'll live. But not for very long if he does things as stupid as that."

The woman's liquid dark eyes arced dark fire. "Weren't you ever a child?"

George nodded. "Yeah. But where I grew up boys knew how to rope wild horses."

She challenged that. "How?"

He turned towards her. She was every bit as beautiful as the painting, and up this close she smelled wonderful; clean and sort of like wildflowers in a mountain meadow.

"You first off make the tag-end of your lariat fast close to the ground around a solid post, either a snubbing post, or if one of those isn't handy, to a stout corral post, *then* you rope the mustang. Then you get the hell out of the way until he's choked himself down." George stopped speaking. The two lads who had been watching him, sidled up a little closer.

One of them said, "Mister," in a piping,

diffident voice, and he was the brave one of the two. "Mister . . . you shot that lariat in two."

George looked down into the upraised, solemn faces. He felt the admiration and the awe, and it made him uncomfortable. "Well," he told the boys, groping for something logical, "I tried to catch hold of the rope but the darned horse was moving too fast."

The other lad, emboldened, said, "I don't think even Ned Colt in my book could have shot like that, mister. I don't think even Jesse James could have —"

George said, "Accident," and reddened because Dorry Sloan was looking from the boys to George, now, with a different expression. "Just an accident. You saw — I had to fire twice."

". . . Right smack in two," murmured one of the boys, and sighed with emerging hero-worship.

George scowled, then turned. Dorry Sloan was gazing at him with an odd look on her face. He shrugged, waiting for her to say something. She didn't speak, and a moment later she turned and walked towards the roadway, bound back in the direction of her dress shop.

"Mister . . ."

George looked down again. "What is it now?"

"Can I have the bullet casing?"

George lifted out his gun, opened the gate, shucked out *both* casings, handed one to each boy, plugged in two fresh loads from the loops in his belt, leathered the ivory-handled Colt, swore under his breath and headed after the beautiful woman, but when he got over across the road again, he turned southward and stamped on down to the saloon for a glass of beer.

CHAPTER SIX: IN THE WAKE OF A HERO

George got a room at the hotel, above the gunshop, but the only reason he was able to get the room was because Harlan Bowman had hired Hank for his drive to Lincoln Lake, which provided a vacancy, otherwise there were no rooms available, according to the grumpy old gunsmith who owned the building.

Hank was gone by the time George hauled his bedroll and saddlebags upstairs, but he had told the gunsmith he'd been hired on by B Bar, and the gunsmith had told George.

The room overlooked the street, which

George only indifferently noticed as he flung his bedroll down atop the bare mattress on the old brass bedstead, and emptied his gatherings atop a table with one short leg, then draped the empty saddlebags over the back of the room's only chair.

The effects of his recent bath were not very lasting; after that sweaty turmoil over across from the dress shop with the wild horse, he was wringing wet again. It hadn't helped much, either, that he'd drunk a beer at the Oxbow; beer, in hot weather, had a tendency to make a man perspire like a horse running uphill. But at least there was a slight breeze coming through his roadway window, and that was more welcome than the big, bearded man who came banging on George's door.

Abe Hepler came into the room so full of humility and gratitude that George almost decided he did not like the blacksmith. In the midst of Hepler's glowing expression of thanks, George said, "You know, if that boy of yours belonged to me, Mr. Hepler, I'd tan his britches."

The blacksmith smiled through his beard. "I'll take care of that maybe next week, but right now he's got a dislocated shoulder from where he hit the post, and his nose is cracked a little. I just wanted you to

60

know, Mr. Lefton, any time you ever need anything, and I can provide it, you just call on me. Except for you, I know for a fact Carl would have been dragged to death."

George was distinctly uncomfortable. "Where did he get that mustang anyway, and how did they ever get him to stay inside that rotten old corral?"

"They bought him for fifty cents from a horsetrader who passed through last weekend, and they never went near him in the corral, except to haul in water and pitch a little hay over the stringers. I *told* them not to get inside the corral with that dad-blasted little runt of a worthless horse. I *told* them and *told* them." Hepler ran a limp, soiled sleeve over his oily face squeezing off sweat. Then he shoved out a big, thick hand. "I'm wholly obliged to you," he said.

George shook, then eased his caller out, closed the door and went over to the window to catch some of the breeze. Downstairs and across the way he saw Shep lope up with another man, a cowboy who was tanned almost as dark as old leather, swing down out front of the saloon, and go stamping on inside. Shep had a new hat, a conventional Stetson with a flat top and a wide brim. Also, he was wearing only a faded old blue shirt, not the claw-hammer preacher's coat.

George decided to go have another beer because he wanted a few words with Shep. He went down the outside stairway and had just stepped off the plankwalk when a man hailed him from the shadows over in front of the gunshop. George turned. It was the scanty-haired old physician, who resembled a hungry sparrow, in some ways. George reluctantly went back into the shade of the wooden overhang.

The doctor said, "Young man, you saved that boy's life."

George studied the older man, and decided that the doctor probably was as inured to things of this nature as anyone could be, and would probably understand how George felt, so he said, "I'll tell you something, Doctor: I'm getting tired of hearing about it."

He was correct, the older man gave his head a quick bird-like up and down shake. "I reckon you are," he said, watching George from bird-bright grey eyes. "Just one thing sticks in my mind, young feller. That was some shooting you did."

George looked up and down the roadway, then back again. "Pure accident, Doctor. Just a pure accident." He smiled. "I've got to see a man over at the bar." He turned and hiked on across the sunblaze and pushed past the Oxbow's doors.

It was cool and gloomy inside; it usually took a moment for a man's eyes to adjust to the gloom after the sunshine. George made out Shep and the tanned rider with him, walked over on Shep's far side and called to Herb Sloan for a beer. The barman stared a moment, then bobbed his head and spoke, something he rarely did when he acknowledged an order. "Coming right up," he called back. George turned. Shep grinned and winked.

"This here is Bowie Jarvis, George. Bowie, this here is my old pardner George Lefton." They nodded across Shep, and George's drink arrived. He put down a coin. Herb Sloan shook his head. "Not today, Mr. Lefton. Drinks for you are on the house today."

Shep's ugly, grinning big face slowly congealed in an expression of astonishment, and as Sloan departed Shep looked down. "What the hell did you do?"

George swore. "Some damned idiot of a kid got hung up in a lariat roping a mustang, and I shot the rope loose is all."

Shep continued to gaze at George, then he got a faint look of anxiety across his face and said no more until the cowboy with him said he had to go out back for a minute and walked away. Then Shep leaned down and growled.

"Why'n hell did you have to go and do that for?"

George drank half his beer before answering. "Would you have let the kid get dragged to death?"

Shep turned his glass in its sticky pool for a moment, then sighed. "I reckon not." He downed the drink. "Maybe they'll figure it was an accident."

"That's what I've been telling everyone. A pure accident. By the way, Hank hired on with B Bar today to make some kind of drive. Bowman of B Bar came looking for you, but we told him you were out of town, so Hank hired on with him."

Shep continued to turn his glass in the puddle atop the bar. "I been helping some boys east of town a few miles make their gather. They're figuring on going up to Battle Mountain, to a bunch of meadows by a lake up there, to summer their cattle." Shep looked at George. "It's going to be a race. They seen B Bar gathering last week, and they commenced too, because this here is a bad drought summer coming on." Shep grinned. "It'll be a race up there. First outfit to make it can claim all the feed. That's the way they've always operated around here." Shep banged the bartop and when Sloan came, glaring at Shep, the big grinning cowboy said, "Two more of the same, friend, whisky for me and beer for my friend here, who ain't been weaned long enough to drink like a he-man." It was a small joke, but Herb Sloan didn't smile as he went away to refill their glasses. Shep watched him depart, then wagged his head. "You know, that feller's feet must hurt him, or something. I've never seen him look cheerful."

George was thinking of something else. "If two cow outfits ride for Battle Mountain, Shep, and only one can get there first . . ." George looked up.

Shep laughed quietly. "Naw, there won't be no trouble, George. These boys all sort of grew up around here together."

George Lefton had seen range wars erupt among men who had grown up together, over a lot less important things than summer feed in a drought country. He said, "Maybe you'd better keep out of it, Shep."

"Well; Hank's helping B Bar ain't he? Why can't I help these other fellers then?"

"Maybe you *both* better keep out of it," stated George.

The tanned rider returned from out back, sidled up close and called for another drink, which ended the private conversation.

A little later, Shep and his new friend drifted out of the saloon, leaving George to finish his last beer of the day alone. Herbert Sloan came over, leaned upon his bar and said, "I talked to Dorry." He said it as though George knew Dorry well. "She told me what happened over yonder with that damned dink horse. She said she was rude to you."

George found this variation on the story of his interruption with the would-be horse-breakers acceptable, but otherwise he was thoroughly tired of hearing about that interlude. He said, "Well, maybe she wasn't. I was a little mad at the kid. He did a real stupid thing and could have got killed. I told her if he'd been my kid I'd have fanned his seat a little."

The black-eyed unsmiling barman nodded. "That's exactly right. That's what I told her. I'd have done the same. Most men would have. She said she didn't really have time to consider anything but the fact that the kid was bleeding, and there you stood, growling at him. She said if I saw you to apologise for her."

George raised his eyes to the painting over

the bar, then he nodded. "All right." He dropped his eyes. "She lit into me like a mother wolf." He smiled. "Anyway, it's over and done with."

Herb Sloan's black, testy gaze lingered. "No," he drawled softly. "No, Mr. Lefton, it's not over. In a place like St. Louis it might be over and forgot by tomorrow, but not out here it won't be. You see, back there men who can shoot like that aren't so terribly rare, but out here they sure as hell are. I'll tell you what I figure; for a few days folks are just going to think you did a really heroic thing. But let them have another week to think about it, and someone's going to come up and ask how it happened that you could shoot like that — breaking the rope on a running horse with one shot."

"Two shots," stated George, and returned Sloan's look. "And I've already told how that happened a dozen times. It was a pure accident, a complete stroke of luck."

Sloan's eyes did not waver. "Maybe. Maybe not. That's how folks are going to figure it; maybe it *was* an accident, and maybe it *wasn't* an accident."

George straightened up off the bar. "They can think what they like, Mr. Sloan," he said, and turned to leave the saloon.

Sloan had one more remark to make. "Mr.

Lefton; three strangers ride into Shafter the same day from three different directions — and one of them can out-shoot anyone we've ever seen around here." Herb Sloan straightened back and made a big swipe with his bar-rag before completing it. "Folk's aren't dumb, you know. They may never come up with the right answer, but they sure as hell are going to come up with the obvious one."

George walked out into the shade of the front walk and considered the drowsy roadway, which was nearly empty this time of day. Great! Hank had worried about *Shep* doing something to tip their hand. And it wasn't Shep at all, it was *George.*

Still, he hadn't been able to do anything else. Unless of course he'd let the damned worthless horse drag the blacksmith's kid to death, which almost certainly would have happened.

He struck off in the direction of the liverybarn to look in on his horse, and made a wide diversion so as not to have to cut across in front of Hepler's shop. He'd had about all the gratitude he could stand for one day.

At the liverybarn an old, muddy-faced hostler was watering down the earthen floor, which was about fifteen feet wide, and which ran on through the barn from front to back. It was cool in there, and no doubt sprinkling the runway had a lot to do with that.

George and the old hostler exchanged a nod, then George went to find his horse. The chestnut gelding was dozing, sleek and lazy and filled out again after his long ride down-country. George looked down. Hank had been right, the chestnut needed new shoes. But he'd be damned if he'd lead the horse up to Hepler's shop. Maybe in a few days, when the blacksmith had got back to being a normal man again, he'd do that, but not today.

He might have taken the horse out for some exercise, even in the heat of the day, except that now he couldn't; if those worn old shoes broke or fell off, the horse's hooves might crack and chip.

He decided to go over to the restaurant and have some food. It was late for dinner and early for supper, which meant that Charley Santee's place probably would be empty, something George anticipated with pleasure. He didn't want one more person to tell him he'd been a hero, ever again as long as he lived.

He was also thinking of something else; those last words Herb Sloan had said, just before George had left the Oxbow: Give folks a week, and they were going to be saying something else about the man who had broken that damned lariat with a pistol shot.

Chapter Seven:
A Stroll By Starlight

There were only two places to eat in Shafter, at home or down at Charley Santee's restaurant. Most folks ate at home. But the ones like George Lefton who had no home to eat at, visited Charley Santee's place whenever the mood struck them, as it did the evening after the interlude with the wild horse when George went in late because his horse had come from Hepler's forge late, and he'd hung around the liverybarn to see that the shoeing job was done the way he wanted it to be done. He hadn't gone down to Hepler's shop, he'd sent the liverybarn day-man in his place.

There was one advantage about eating late, you not only didn't get some high-flyer's elbow along a crowded counter, but you were likely to get better service. At least that's the way it worked at Charley Santee's place, and after a few inadvertent late meals, George had just about decided he would be late every night.

But the place had two customers when George entered. One was a narrow-shouldered wispy man whom George did not recognise from the back, and really did not look very closely at in any case as he went on up to the counter, and the second customer was on the far side of the wispy man and was a woman, probably the wispy man's wife, something else George did not speculate about as Charley came padding along in the bedroom slippers he wore all the time, instead of shoes or boots.

Charley beamed. He had formed a strong liking for George Lefton. In fact, Charley had liked him even before the interlude with the wild horse, but since then Charley, the only local man who could honestly say he and George were friends prior to that event, basked a little in reflected glory. When the banker had asked him the day before if Charley had known George Lefton was such a deadly shot with a handgun, Charley did not overlook this opportunity to talk down to the banker.

"Why sure I knew," he'd said. "Anybody could tell that; didn't you see them ivory grips on his gun? You never see fellers wearing them that don't take pride in their weapons."

But tonight, as Charley brought George's

meal and coffee, except for the big, broad smile, Charley Santee was circumspect. His liking was tempered with respect, after that business of shooting the lariat rope apart, and a respected man is treated with slightly more deference than just a friend is treated.

Charley had baked a green apple pie that afternoon. He brought forth a big slice of that to go along with the elk steak, fried spuds and coffee, and when George saw him hovering and braced for the inevitable comments about the wild horse episode, Charley was called away to take the money of the wispy man at the far end of his counter, and George got a reprieve.

He did not even look down there. The food was good and he was hungry, and despite Charley Santee's personal appearance, and the plain, almost drab appearance of his hole-in-the-wall cafe, Charley was really a very good cook — when he wanted to be and took the time to be.

George was reaching for his cup when someone said, "My father always told me snap judgements were usually wrong."

He looked up and around. Dorry Sloan was smiling. Beside her, the wispy man was looking at his watch; it was the doctor. Before George could comment the doctor snapped his watch-case closed and said,

"Well; I think I've allowed just about enough time. If you folks'll excuse me I've got to go deliver a baby." The doctor briskly nodded, turned and briskly left the restaurant. He never seemed to do anything casually.

George smiled up into the beautiful woman's face. "This is good coffee," he said. "Care to join me in a cup?"

Dorry hesitated; she had just finished dinner but Charley Santee beamed as he turned to get another cup, so she sat down, faced forward and did not watch as George went back to his meal. When the coffee arrived Charley went to clear away the plates at the lower end of his counter, and George spoke without turning.

"Your pappy was right."

Dorry laughed softly. "You are a very opinionated man, aren't you?"

George had to ponder that before answering. "Maybe. About some things I reckon I am." He finished and looked at the apple pie.

Dorry said, "If you don't eat it, Charley's feelings will be hurt."

George picked up his fork and went to work on the pie. He tucked it away and washed it down with the last of his coffee, feeling as loaded as a tick. He grinned. "Now Charley can sleep peacefully tonight and I'll pitch and toss for over-eating. But it was good pie."

"Charley's a good cook. I thought about opening a cafe here in Shafter, but when I got to know the competition, I gave it up."

George looked at her. "You're not a good cook?"

She got momentarily flustered. "Well; I can *cook,* Mr. Lefton, but there's more to it than that."

George thought he understood: Charley, the broken-down old cowboy, had his little business and his prized self-respect. George said, "Sure there is." He looked over his shoulder out of the window at the starbright night. "I'll walk you home, ma'am."

She was agreeable and arose. George dumped some silver atop the counter, winked at Charley, got back a wink, and walked out into the night with Dorry Sloan.

There was a little activity up at the Oxbow, and over at the gunshop some men who belonged to the township volunteer fire department were either tuning up some musical instruments, or were playing some kind of music, but not very well.

A few other strollers were abroad, over across the roadway. Usually, people did not use the east side of the road for night-strolling because up around the Oxbow men were constantly coming and going, and also usually, they were happy, beered-up cowboys who could almost be counted upon to make unnecessary remarks when girls walked past in the evening.

But this did not trouble George, as he and Dorry took their time. He was thinking of other things. So was she, evidently, because she said, "Herb told me what he said to you today — about people beginning to wonder how you happened to shoot that lariat apart. He's right, you know, Mr. Lefton. They *are* going to talk."

George listened to the noise up at the saloon as he said, "They talk anyway, don't they? If it's not about me, it's about someone else." He smiled over at her. "Directly, something else will pop up and they'll forget me."

She moved leisurely at his side, looking down. Clearly, something was bothering her. He studied her profile then said, "Get it out of your craw; what is it?"

"*I'm* curious too," she retorted, lifting her head to him.

He looked at her soft-lighted face, thought a moment, then said, "All right; ask away."

"How did you get that good with a gun?"

"Practice. Lots of men who've had to be off cow-hunting by themselves for days at a time, practice with their guns. There's precious little else to do. If you think I'm a gunfighter or something like that, you're wrong." They came almost abreast of the saloon. "I once knew a feller who learned to braid and plait, and another one who took along needles and yarn and came back with as nice a big woolly sweater as you ever saw." He grinned at her look of incredulity.

She said, "You mean, he knitted it?"

"Yup. Like I told you, when a man's off by himself for long periods at a time, maybe winter feeding or stray hunting, he'd surely better have some kind of a hobby, or come springtime he'll be as loco as jay-bird."

She seemed to accept this explanation. He had seemed sincere, and in fact he *was* sincere because he had been telling her the absolute truth.

They passed the saloon and came even with the darkened bank with its forbidding big steel shutters barred for the night across the front door and both front windows. The light cast outward from the saloon dwindled again, up the northerly plankwalk. Dorry said, "But you see, you're a stranger here, and people aren't going to know you've been a rangerider who made a hobby out of practising with his guns, are they?"

He guessed her point. "So they're going

to think I'm Jesse James junior, is that it?"

She smiled. "You're not old enough to be Jesse James junior. How about one of the Earps over in Arizona?"

He looked, saw the smile, and slid easily into a matching mood. "All right. George Earp?"

"Huh-huh."

"Lefton Earp?"

"That's worse."

He watched her. When she was easy with someone she seemed younger than she had to be. He did not try to guess her age, but he thought she would be maybe five or six years younger than he was. They strolled along, comfortable with one another. He was very conscious of her beside him, but she did not act at all conscious of him, at least not in the same way.

"I told Herb you and your friends were simply riders drifting in for the seasonal work," she said, and cocked her head at him. "He said all the rangemen who wanted to work had already arrived and had either been hired, or had ridden off looking elsewhere for work. It's too late in the season, he told me. Is that true?"

George was not a man who ordinarily took personal questions very well. But this was different, and even though he felt a little annoyed with her, he answered calmly enough. "It's not true, because all rangemen don't just jump out of bed one morning, saddle up and all go riding north the same day. Some riders like to hunt out new country. Some get a late start. Some quit one ranch and go drifting around looking for a better outfit to work for. There are hundreds of them on the loose all summer long, with a hundred different reasons for wandering."

"Which are you, Mr. Lefton; why are you wandering?"

They were almost to the front of her little building. "Change of scenery," he told her without lying. "Looking for a place to settle down, I reckon." He stopped with her at the dress shop door. It was dark up there at the north end of town. "Now *you* tell *me* something, Dorry Sloan: Why are you burying yourself in a place like Shafter?"

She looked up smiling again. "Your reason will do; looking for something. That's why we came out west from St. Louis. To find a place to breathe."

"Shafter?" he asked, and she nodded.

"Shafter. But — it isn't paradise, Mr. Lefton."

He sensed her mood and her thoughts. "I doubt if there is such a place." He grinned.

"At least not in New Mexico, and I can tell you for a fact it's not in Arizona either . . . But maybe people have to make their own paradise."

She looked searchingly into his face. "You're not just a rangerider, Mr. Lefton. I've met my share of cowboys out here — and ranchers. They aren't like you."

He said, "Dorry, if you brought high hopes from St. Louis and got 'em stomped on out here, don't blame New Mexico. No two places I've ever been are alike. If a person is going to stay in one place, he'd better set his sights no higher, and no lower, than that one place. Shafter sure isn't St. Louis or Chicago or New York, but then you and Herb left the east out of choice, so don't expect whatever you liked about things back there to be the same out here."

He stepped past, tried the door, found it unlocked and opened it for her. As he turned she was looking at him with her head slightly cocked again, her expression quizzical. "As I said, you're different from the others."

He raised a hand, tipped up her head, kissed her softly, pulled back and smiled. "Lady, so are you. Good night."

"Good night."

He started back down towards the Oxbow,

but stepped off the plankwalk before he got that far down and went on an angling course towards the gunshop, and his room upstairs above it. Thankfully, the volunteer firemen had ceased their practising for the night. The noise from the Oxbow, however, did not diminish for another couple of hours, but that kind of a racket George was accustomed to; he had been hearing it most of his life in one cow town or another.

He got ready for bed, then leaned out the upstairs window, savouring the faint, cool breeze that rode above the rooftops, rode through the high treetops and brought the acrid-sweet scent of sage and chaparral, grass and hot earth, from far out over the eastward range.

She was, he told himself, something that tugged at a man's innermost spirit even in soft memory. Charley Santee had been right, George Lefton had never seen a woman like her before in his life.

CHAPTER EIGHT: AN UNEVENTFUL DAY IN TOWN

Hank and John Bowman came to town in the old buckboard for supplies the next morning, early. George saw them from the doorway of Santee's restaurant as he was leaving after breakfast, and walked on up. John went into the store with B Bar's list, but Hank saw George coming, and waited, wearing a pleasant smile.

"You haven't located yet?" he asked, as George walked up to him. "You ought to ride out and hunt a job. This is pretty good country, George."

George had no fault to find with the country, and he didn't get a chance to answer Hank's first question.

"We're victualling for the drive up to Lincoln Lake," explained Hank. "Head out about dawn tomorrow. By the way, have you seen Shep lately?"

George shook his head. "Nope." Then he said what he had observed thus far about his friend. "You look happy and sassy. B Bar must agree with you."

"Good outfit," conceded Hank. "You know, I've been thinking; a man could do a lot worse than to take up some land around here and bring in a little herd to start out with."

George thought that over. "Yeah, I reckon he could — and providing he was real careful and didn't start out too big all at once, and make everyone wonder about him, he could probably make it just fine."

Hank winked. "I know about that. I've

been thinking on it the last few days." Hank glanced past the doorway of the general store. "I'd better get in there and lend Johnny a hand." He gazed steadily at George a moment. "Get out and around, George; believe me, there are a hell of a lot worse places for a man to settle in and put down roots." He winked again, and turned to hasten into the store.

George went down by the liverybarn quietly smiling to himself. Hank had always been a sceptical, restless man who did not find much to laugh about or to admire in life. Today was the first time George had ever seen him in a sustained mood of self-satisfaction. No question about it, Hank Burton had found his niche, finally.

He did not see Hank and the younger Bowman pull out of town. He got buttonholed by the liveryman who had a pet peeve about either having to cobble together his own saddles, bridles and harnesses, or buy new ones, which he said was not only exorbitant, but was also a dirty shame, because a town as large as Shafter not only needed a harness shop, but deserved one.

By the time George got away from his indignant acquaintance and headed back towards the centre of town, not only was the buckboard gone, but there were four horses tied out front of the Oxbow that hadn't been there earlier. One of those horses was a sleek, handsome thoroughbred. George started up in that direction.

He almost bumped into the doctor, who was leaving his office, black satchel in hand, hat upon the back of his head, looking pre-occupied. George side-stepped to avoid the collision and the doctor, flustered, gave a quick, rough apology.

"Sorry, son, sorry. Wasn't thinking where I was going." He looked up at George a moment, then said, "Abe Hepler's boy is coming along just fine. I reckon the best part of having your right shoulder in a cast is that you don't have to do any writing or 'rithmetic at school." Doc grinned. "Buy you a drink this evening if I'm back in time. Someone at one of the ranches south of town thinks there's an epidemic of some kind down there. I'll tell you what *I* think: If ranchers worked more when they should be working, and spent less time making stills and putting up their own whisky, there'd be a lot fewer epidemics."

As the doctor went briskly away in the direction of the liverybarn, where he kept his horse and buggy, George chuckled and continued on up to the saloon, pushed inside and saw Shep at the bar with three bronzed, capable-looking rangemen. Shep caught sight of George and turned with a whoop, left his companions and, grabbing George's arm, took him to a little table at the north end of the room, up near the big, pot-bellied iron stove that kept the place warm in wintertime.

As they sat down Shep leaned, whisky glass in hand, dropped his voice to a conspiratorial whisper and said, "There's an old boy working at one of the ranches I been chousing horses for over east of town, who's from my old stomping grounds in Texas. His name's Billy Ray Tolbert. Maybe you heard me talk about Billy Ray sometime. I knew him when we was kids. Anyway, one of the ranches down home is on the block. Billy Ray got that in a letter from his sister down there."

George shook his head when Herb passed by; he didn't want a drink. Herb returned to his bar and George said, "Shep, you go back to Texas and plunk down a big wad of money and someone is going to want to know where you got it."

Shep smiled broadly, fished in his pocket and dug out three large nuggets of California gold. "That's where, old son. I got this all figured out. That's why I bought the nuggets off a Mex *vaquero* who was working east of town as wrangler for one of the cow outfits. He quit to go back to Messico; got home-sick or something. I bought these here nuggets off him. They're worth a heap of money, George. I figure to take them back to Texas with me to show around. I already told Billy Ray I prospected in the Mother Lode country in California, and showed him the nuggets. He swallered it hook line and sinker. He's going back with me." Shep returned the gold to his pocket. "Pardner; us Texans are different from most folks. We just don't thrive very well any-where but in Texas."

George laughed. His personal and private opinion agreed that Texans only belonged in Texas; most other places found them too noisy, too overbearing, and too obnoxious. George had known a lot of them, and with but very few exceptions he'd tolerated them without ever really liking them. Shep had been one of those exceptions, but George had no illusions on that score either; he'd had a steady dose of Shep before their rob-bery of the Laramie bank, and Shep had started getting on his nerves too.

The only bit of advice he could offer, he gave out with now. "Be damned careful, Shep. If they get any one of us, they're sure as hell going to be able to back-track and get the rest of us."

Shep leaned back, downed his whisky and looked raffishly at George. "Old pardner, never you worry. They'll get nothing from me, not even though they drag me ahind wild horses."

"When are you hauling out?"

Shep leaned upon the table again, turning thoughtful. "Damned if I rightly know. I'm sort of bound to help those fellers I been riding with, trail their critters up into the mountains, so maybe not until that's done with."

George pricked up his ears. "When are they going to head out?"

Shep wasn't sure. "Two, three days, I expect. The gathering is just about all finished. They got to send in a wagon tomorrow for supplies, and we got a lot of horses to shoe yet. I'd guess maybe day after tomorrow."

George nodded stoically. He was in the middle, but in any event he wouldn't have told either Hank nor Shep the other's plans.

Shep stood up. "Come on over and have one little drink with me'n the boys, then we got to get back. We was over near town looking for strays and figured we'd just sort of sneak in and hoist a couple."

They went to the bar and George turned

down the whisky and asked Herb for a beer, then the little group of them discussed a lot of things, the drying ranges, the prospects for saving rains, a herd of wild horses someone had seen in the mountains northeast of Shafter, and finally, when the cowboys were ready to depart, they all went out front and Shep, the last one to duck under to the tie-rack, leaned and hurriedly whispered. "I'll see you and Hank before I haul out."

George watched the riders lope north to the end of town then swing eastward. They had barely cleared the end of town when a stage came rattling through. It would stop down at the little way-station located between Hepler's shop and the liverybarn. There was usually a change of hitches down there, but not always because the north-south coaches did not operate on a very tight schedule; there was seldom any purpose in pushing the horses hard, so quite often one hitch of four head took the stages on southward as well. Down there, it was all flat, open country anyway, and caused no strain or fatigue on a hitch.

George did as most people in a cow town did; in any small town for that matter; when a coach arrived in town, he stood out front of the saloon leaning upon an overhang upright watching the passengers alight.

There were two drummers, each with his sample cases, and there was a harassed looking young woman, as plain as a mud fence, trying to cope with two spoiled children, a little boy and a little girl. The last passenger to climb out was a lanky, nut-brown man wearing a creased dark hat of the kind cowmen wore farther north. He stood aloof from the others and cast a slow look all around before passing on inside the stage depot.

An old man limped out with a lard bucket and a broad wooden ladle to apply axle and hub grease. When he'd finished that, he went around the hitch inspecting harness, horse's shoes, and finally the coach's running-gear. The last thing he did was take the horses off the pole and water them two at a time.

George turned as Herb came forth behind him and said, "The mail is in."

George wasn't interested. He saw the harassed, thin woman come back out herding her troublesome youngsters like a worried mother-hen, and thought back to his own boyhood; if he'd acted like that, when he'd got home his father would have taken him to the woodshed, and if he didn't, George's mother would have.

Herb stood chewing a cigar, his dark eyes fixed upon the lanky man with the crease in his hat. "Lawman," he muttered around the cigar. "I can smell them this far away."

George's interest quickened. The lanky stranger came forth and stood, hipshot, thumbs hooked in his shellbelt, looking the town over. His hat was tipped back, his stance was relaxed, and George got the impression that whoever the stranger was, he was not too impressed with Shafter.

Abe Hepler, down in front of his shop, also watching, turned back to his work inside. Evidently he hadn't seen anyone arrive on the coach that intrigued him. But tomorrow he'd come to the doorway all the same, and more than likely, he still wouldn't find anything that would interest him.

Herb removed his cigar, spat, then turned back into the saloon. He too, had seen all he wanted to see.

George kept an eye upon the man with the crease in his hat. Maybe Herb had been right, but to George the lanky man looked like a rangerider, a cowman, maybe a horse or mule buyer, and maybe even a cattle contractor. Of just one thing did George feel positive, whatever the stranger did for a living, he did it out of doors.

Finally, the coach had its same horses

latched back on the pole, tugs hanging slack, and the stationmaster, who always wore a green eyeshade, summer or winter, came forth officiously to check his passenger and manifest list against the load. While he was doing this the old hostler retreated around behind the building with his lard pail and wooden ladle. He did not even look at the passengers. As far as he was concerned, he had just earned his day's keep, and until the next coach arrived, perhaps later tonight, or perhaps the following morning early, he could spend his time in the shade out back trying to patch harness, something he was not good at at all, but something which allowed him solitude, and he was old enough to appreciate solitude, when it could be ameliorated a little with a bottle of lion sweat kept well hidden under a pile of ancient grain sacks.

George did not move until the passengers were climbing back aboard. He waited. The last one to climb in was the lanky man with the creased hat, and for a bad moment or two George wasn't sure that he would get in. But he did, after the harassed woman had shooed her children inside. The stationmaster closed the door, the whip looked down, got the nod, whistled, cracked his long, silver-ferruled drover's lash, the horses leaned into their collars, and the stage lurched ahead.

The only real day-to-day contact Shafter had with the outside world was pulling away in a light skiff of pale dust. When the dust settled back, so would Shafter, until tomorrow when the next coach arrived.

George heaved a sigh and turned to go down to Charley Santee's place for something to eat. Then he thought he'd take his chestnut horse out for some exercise. The worst thing in the world for a horseman — because it was preventable — was asotoeria; when a man's horse came down with that, he was shamed in the eyes of all other horsemen. George had never had it happen and did not intend for it to ever happen, not to him, and not to his chestnut horse.

CHAPTER NINE: AN AFTERNOON'S RIDE

George felt the heat, something that usually did not bother him much, and decided the reason he felt it now was because he'd been doing nothing but hang around town in the shade for a couple of weeks. Maybe Hank's advice about getting out more, was worth something after all. He rode out over B Bar range for several miles, until the sun was dropping and reddening, then he turned northward and loped out the chestnut horse for a mile or so, and finally, when he had the stageroad in sight, he saw another rider, the first one he'd seen all afternoon. A freight wagon riding on chalks someone had lashed to the springs because it was overloaded, had crept past, but otherwise George had seen no one, so he watched this particular horseman — and got a surprise when the rider left the stageroad and headed for him.

He conjectured that it was a stranger to the Battle Mountain country, who had seen George and had decided to get some directions from him. It wouldn't have been a bad guess under other circumstances, but when the rider loped closer George hauled up, leaned atop his saddlehorn because he did not believe his eyes, and when Dorry came the last hundred yards he eased back and sighed. It had never once occurred to him that she might own a horse or ride one.

She smiled. She was bare-headed. Her black hair, like her eyes, made a strong contrast to her peaches-and-cream complexion. She was riding astride, which wasn't altogether unusual, but in most places east of the Missouri it wasn't considered nice or ladylike. She wore her man's blue workshirt well. So well, in fact, that this was how George first identified the oncoming rider as a female instead of a male. She had small, silver-inlaid Southwestern spurs on her boots.

"Are you lost?" she said gaily.

George returned her smile. "Nope. But I'd have bet a good horse you'd be the last person I'd meet out here today."

She drew rein. "Why today?"

"It's hot," he said, simply.

"It's always hot this time of year. Anywhere, it's hot. I like it."

He considered that. "You like the heat?"

"Yes. Don't you?"

He thought a moment. "If you like it, then there can't be anything wrong with it." He turned his horse. "Going back now?"

She was. "Yes. I just couldn't stay inside another moment, so I saddled up and lit out about noon, rode part way up the pass, then turned back." She looked over enquiringly. "That's a beautiful horse. I've seen him before at the livery barn. Did you raise him?"

George looked down. "Me? Raise a horse? No'm, and no one else raises horses, if they use them much. There's always someone else foolish enough to do that. All a man has to do is wait; sooner or later he'll find some horse-rancher or some cowboy, or some trader, who is hard up. Then you buy your horse cheap and the other feller's lost all that time raising and breaking it."

"What a heartless way to be," she said, dark eyes laughing at him. She raised an arm. "I saw a big cloud of dust over west of here, when I was up the pass. B Bar must be moving cattle."

George thought about that too. If B Bar was indeed moving cattle, they were doing it a day earlier than Hank had said they meant to trail out for the high country.

Dorry dropped her arm. "I thought I'd see you last night at Charley's cafe," she said, and when he looked at her, she did not turn away.

"I come in late, usually, because it's not so crowded," he explained. "That way I also get a lot of gossip from Charley. Say; we're going to get back late this evening. I'll stand you to a dinner."

She didn't hesitate. "All right. But I'm very hungry. I may bankrupt you."

"If anyone's got to do, I'd sure rather it'd be you," he said, and twisted in the saddle at a rearward sound.

Another freight outfit was coming down to the flat country. As George and Dorry watched the driver and swamper set up, climbed down and unlashed the skid made of chain and a big thick sapling, so that the rear wheels could turn again.

George said, "You know, that's a hard way to make a living, freighting in mountainous country."

Dorry caught his head turning back. "What *do* you want to do for a living? I see you around town all the time. Your two friends have gone to work."

He stared a moment, then stood in the stirrups and got re-settled astride the saddle before answering. She'd caught him completely off-guard. If *she* was beginning to wonder, so were other people. He spoke off the top of his mind, but it wasn't actually something he hadn't toyed with a little, recently.

"What do you think of a saddle and harness works in Shafter?" he asked.

She rode a dozen or so yards before answering. Then she said, "Can you make saddles?"

He fidgeted. "Well; lord knows I've mended enough harness all my life, and I've made some bridles and pack outfits and the like."

She persisted. "Saddles?"

He confessed that he couldn't. "Never made one in my life." He looked over. "But

95

I was thinking that maybe the harness work would tide me over until I learned." He waited, and when she didn't answer, he said, "Well . . . ?"

She raised liquid dark eyes. "You could do it, I know that. The question is — do you really want to?"

He sighed and shook his head at her. "Damn it, Dorry, you cut right through to the tender place every time."

She smiled. "Care to hear my guesswork about you?"

He fidgeted again; he did not particularly want to hear anyone's guesswork about him, but least of all *her* guesswork. He was beginning to worry a little, because she thought like a man, something he'd never before encountered in a woman.

When he did not reply she spoke anyway. "You're still a wanderer, George. You're still looking for something. If you opened a shop here, it might just be that you were doing it because you felt you had to do *something*."

He took that up. "I *do* have to do something."

She led him along as though he were a child. "All right; do you like Shafter?"

"Yes."

"The Battle Mountain Country?"

"Yes."

"Do you like working with leather indoors?"

He'd always liked working with leather.
Working indoors he wasn't so sure about,
so he temporised. "I've always been pretty
good with my hands. I like making things
and I like leather."

She looked ahead where the town lay in
the soft gloaming. Perhaps she'd missed the
part he'd left out, and maybe she hadn't,
but in any event she said, "There is a vacant
store next to the general store. It would be
ideal for a harness shop, I think. Everyone
goes to the general store; if you had a sign
up right next door . . ." She looked at him.
"Are you going to do it?"

He had an odd feeling that she was some-
how or other bulldogging him into this, but
maybe, he told himself, it was simply that
she wanted him to start *something,* anything
at all rather than to continue loafing, and
he really couldn't fault that, even though
he'd been pretty leisurely about definite
things in his own thinking, up to now.

He sighed, looked askance at her, and
when she laughed at his hang-dog expression, he laughed with her. "Yeah, I'm going
to do it," he said.

She was pleased. "I'll help you all I can."
As though she expected a sceptical look,

she rushed on. "I'm good with patterns and layouts and measurements. Isn't that mostly what leather working is, layouts and so forth?"

He nodded. "Yeah, I'll have to find a leather supplier and get tools and all."

She turned brisk, now. "I know most of the salesmen who come through. I can probably help there too."

He looked at her and believed implicitly that salesmen would come by her shop, even the ones who did not peddle the things she would handle. "Who owns that vacant store?" he asked.

She smiled. "My brother. I'll talk to him if you'd like."

He drew back a big breath. "Listen, Dorry, just *help,* don't *boss.*"

She bit her lip and he felt like he'd just kicked a puppy. He tried to overcome this without yielding anything. "I want your help. Honestly. In fact without that I just wouldn't care whether . . ." The situation was getting away from him and he knew it the moment she turned her liquid soft eyes to him. He cleared his throat. "I'm sorry if I hurt your feelings. Only —"

"I understand, George." She wasn't angry, she didn't even act indignant. "Do you know what happens to people who live by themselves too long? They get bossy from necessity and habit. *You* talk to Herb." She smiled. "Tonight?"

He studied her. "You *are* kind of bossy, aren't you?" he said, and they both laughed

The shadows were down, finally, by the time they reached the back-alley leading down the west side of town to the livery-barn. When they turned in and the night-man saw them entering together, his jaw dropped, he leaned slackly upon his pitch-fork, and only George's back, set squarely so that Dorry wouldn't see the man's look, kept her from noticing that she and George had just given someone food for gossip.

When George turned, the nightman scuttled forward to take their reins. George scowled, and led Dorry on through to the yonder roadway. As they strolled up the east-side plankwalk in the darkness provided by the wooden awnings above, he glanced towards the saloon. It was quiet for a change, but the lamps were all lit. Maybe it was a trifle early for the high-jinks to start. Then too, this was the middle of the week; mostly, cowmen and their riders did not show up until Saturday night.

It had slipped his mind that he had asked her to dinner at the restaurant until they were almost to the dress shop, then she said,

"I'll change and meet you down there." He nodded, but his eyes were blank for a moment, something she did not see in the darkness, fortunately.

Outside the dress shop she turned and smiled upwards. "It was a very pleasant ride. I'd like to do it again."

He looked at her in the warm night. Even in a man's old blue workshirt, boots and spurs, she was round and vibrant and wonderful. He remembered how he'd felt the night before when he'd stood by his upstairs window; she had a way of reaching across distances to him, whether they were great distances or, like now, small distances.

He stood there *thinking* all these things, and more, without opening his mouth, until she finally turned to reach for the door, then he said, "Dorry . . ." She turned back in a supple, smooth movement. He still didn't know what to say, but he reached with both arms. She did not exactly yield to him, but she did not step back either. He ran both hands up her arms, then clamped down a little and swayed her forward.

The kiss was soft, like warm velvet. She was not stiff, nor did she loosen against him, but after a moment she did raise her arms to his shoulders, but by then the kiss was finished.

Afterwards, he hung there facing her. She seemed to understand because she smiled, placed both palms against him and said, "It won't take me long."

He would have waited, but she shook her head, so he left her and walked thoughtfully on down past the Oxbow, which was just beginning to liven up, and all the way down to Charley's restaurant. He'd barely cleared the front door when Charley, emerging from the back room, padded over and beamed. There were no other diners along the counter.

"Supper for two?" he asked.

George stared at him. "Where did you get that idea?"

Santee's grin widened to its limit. "Hugh was just in here."

George went over to the counter, dropped down and pushed back his hat. "Who the hell is Hugh?"

"Nightman at the liverybarn," replied Charley, and went padding after a cup of coffee.

George said, "Oh," and slouched forward upon the counter. "Yeah, supper for two. Only she won't be along for a few minutes."

Charley brought back the coffee, still beaming. George tried not to look at him. For once, he'd have welcomed one of Charley's stories about the fight up at the base of Battle Mountain.

Chapter Ten:
The Arrangement

After they had eaten and had managed to get out from under Charley Santee's insipid sighs and eye-rolling looks, they walked up beyond town a short distance on the empty stage road, and up there, without really planning it, George suddenly found her in his arms, her hands against his shoulders, her body yielding to him the full length.

He did not get back to his own room over the gunshop until after midnight. In fact, when he left her at the dress shop and walked back, his footfalls sounded very loud in all the late-night hush that had settled over the rest of the town. Only two lights were still burning; one pair of coach lamps, on each side of the liverybarn entrance guttered and smoked.

George did not drop right off, either, the way he usually did after a long day, he lay awake looking out the roadway window at the far stars and the cobalt sky.

Eventually he dropped off but when he awakened, late, he did not recall when he'd even closed his eyes. He probably wouldn't have awakened when he did, except that a dog-fight erupted downstairs out front of the gunshop, and several men, yelling and swearing, including the grumpy old gun-smith, pitching water upon the fighting animals, awakened him. He went to the window just in time to see three bucketsful of water hit the dogs simultaneously. It was just too much water, the dogs broke away like drowned rats and fled in opposite directions. George went back to get dressed.

The sun was high, Shafter was busy, and before he got downstairs to the washroom, the stage had come and gone. Also, the heat was building, and this time it was coming from the ground up, instead of from the sky down; that meant the last vestiges of spring were truly past and full summer was upon the land. There was not a cloud in the sky, the land began to parch, and when a little wind blew, dust-devils sprang to life. For a fact, it was indeed going to be a drought summer.

George had a late breakfast down at Charley Santee's place, and this time it was not by design. When Charley looked as though he might say something personal, George skewered him with a stony look, and Charley's wind eased out a little at a time. All he said was that the stage driver and guard had come over for a bite to eat before heading on southward, and they had seen a cattle drive coming upland from the north country, which was unusual.

George was only half listening; he was a man who had been transported into a softly warm world of love by way of a woman's arms the night before. Such a thing almost invariably made the matter of returning to the mundane day-to-day rangecountry existence, a reluctant and difficult process.

Even when Charley leaned upon the counter and said, "No cowmen from the north got any right on the Battle Mountain meadows," George only half heard. "It's never happened before, neither," went on Charley. "But this here is a bad summer. I'll tell you what I predict: B Bar's going to get up there, then them trespassing strangers are going to arrive up there — and there is going to be bad trouble." Charley reared back looking indignant. "It won't be the first range war they've had around these parts."

George looked up. "Range war?"

Charley scowled. "You didn't hear a damned thing I said, did you?"

George reached for his coffee cup. "Say it again."

Charley Santee obliged. Then he went over and got himself a cup of coffee and returned, eyeing George speculatively. "One of your pardners is ridin' with B Bar ain't he? Well; if B Bar don't have no idea they are going to run into some northerly cow oufit up there, you might have to be his pall bearer."

George finished his coffee, finished his breakfast, asked where Charley had picked up his information about a strange cow outfit driving for the uplands, and after he got his answer he left and went down to the liverybarn for his horse.

But George did not head northwest to try and overtake B Bar. What had occurred to him, was that if Shep's friends from east of town also started for the uplands, there really could be a war, a three-sided one, and the reasonable thing to do was prevent this, if he could, by stopping at least one drive before it got started.

He did not know the east-range outfits, in fact he'd hardly explored over in that direction at all, but he found Shep without any trouble at all, or, more accurately, Shep found him.

He was loping across a wide bench of curing grass with a faint scent of roiled dust in his nostrils, when two riders came up out of an arroyo up ahead and halted when they saw him behind them. One of those riders called something over to his companion, and the second man spurred on away. The man who had done the calling then turned, descended into the arroyo again, and clambered up the near side of it to sit waiting until George loped up. It was Frank Shepherd, and he looked puzzled.

"Hey, George," he sang out. "What are you doing out here in the heat of the day?"

George reined up and swung to earth to stand in horse-shade. "Trouble coming," he told Shep. "There's a big cow outfit driving upland towards the Battle Mountain range from northward, on the far side of the mountains."

Shep dismounted slowly. "They can't do that," he said, in drawled protest. "That there country belongs to these fellers over here."

"That's my point," stated George. "B Bar is already on the move. Your friends will be on the move in a day or two. If all three outfits get up there about the same time, Shep, there's going to be hell to pay. My guess is that those outsiders driving down from the north know damned well that Battle Mountain country is the reserve range for these cowmen over on this side, and knowing that, but still willing to usurp it, they're coming prepared for trouble."

Shep pushed back his hat, screwed up his face, and stared a long time at George. "B Bar's already on the way?"

"Left this morning before sunup."

"Well, hell," complained Shep, "that means my friends can't make it first, don't it?"

George shrugged. "I'd think so, but I don't know the country up there nor the trails."

"Did you know B Bar was going to get the jump on us, George?"

"Look, Shep, what you told me and what Hank told me, wasn't anything I could give back to either one of you, and you know it. You both put me in the middle, so all I could do was keep my mouth shut. Right?"

Shep hooked both thumbs in his shellbelt while he turned this over in his mind, then, reluctantly, he nodded. "I reckon so. But I been workin' my tail off for nothing, then."

"You're going to work it off some more," exclaimed George. "Go tell your friends B Bar is already on the way. Then tell them about the trespassers coming in from the north. Then meet me over where B Bar is making its drive."

Shep pondered this too, for a long time. Eventually, catching a glimmer of what George had in mind, he nodded his head ponderously. "I reckon you're right. Okay; but maybe I'd better recruit a few hands to come along, if that trespassin' outfit happens to be loaded for bear with extra riders."

George said, "Nope. No battle, Shep."

"Even if we're going to be out-numbered, George?"

"But not out-smarted," said Lefton, and turned back to mount up. "We'll pick up Hank from the B Bar, then the three of us, travelling alone and faster, will get up there to Battle Mountain and stake a claim."

Shep's face screwed up into a hard look of scepticism. "Just the three of us?"

"Yeah, just the three of us. Like I said, we've been out-numbered before, but not out-smarted."

Shep suddenly smiled. "All right. I understand now." He stepped aboard his horse and laughed. "I'll see you wherever B Bar's raisin' dust. Maybe it'll take most of the day, but I'll get up there."

They parted riding in opposite directions. George did not ride fast, it was too hot for that, but he rode steadily, which saved his horse's strength.

He did not really have to hasten in any case; one of the slowest-travelling things under the sun was a cattle drive, particularly if there were young calves. Not *small* calves, but young calves, meaning between two and six months old calves. *Small* calves, meaning baby calves a month old or under, were usually trailed until they played out, then were tossed into a wagon.

But B Bar did not have any small calves; B Bar calved out early, usually in February, and this was early summer so most of the calves, while young, were sturdy enough to make the trip; they just weren't long enough legged to keep up, and their mothers hung back to stay with them, which made the entire drive a slow, almost a monotonous trip.

There was no real occasion to hurry, though. At least as far as B Bar knew, there was no need, and that made a little problem — not for B Bar, but for George; as Shep had noted, you usually found a drive by the great pall of dust. A meandering drive made no dust at all, especially across grassland. George had another handicap; he did not know the range, nor the route a B Bar drive would take.

He rode for two solid hours trying to catch sight of movement or dust, and the last half hour of that time he rode most of the distance standing in his stirrups to get a better sighting.

How he happened to finally pick up B Bar's trail was when something shiny made one dazzlingly brilliant flash. It came and went in a second but George saw it and headed towards the northerly end of the open range.

Finally, his horse picked up the scent of both cattle and other horses. After that, George let the horse take his own trail. An hour later he smelled the drive, then saw it.

Evidently B Bar had not halted for noon. It was a long distance from the headquarters ranch to the foothills and where George saw the wave of red backs and horned heads was almost to the trees, a distance which could only have been covered by steady, slow driving.

George guessed that the Bowmans wanted their cattle into the shady forest before the breathless afternoon heat hit. It was good cowman-strategy.

The closer he got the more noticeable was the odour. It was not unpleasant; the odour of meat-eaters is almost invariably unpleasant, but not grass and browse-eaters. He swung slightly northward so as to intercept the three drag riders. Other horsemen, upon both sides of the drive, were scattered forward, but most of the older cows had some inkling of their ultimate destination, at least they seemed to have the way they swung along up into the trees without a look backwards. Maybe they just smelt the shade, but whatever it was, they headed correctly and therefore needed very little guidance.

There had to be a point rider somewhere up ahead, but George did not see him. Probably because he had already pushed on up through the trees, making trail for the lead animals to follow.

Those men George had been watching, turned. They had seen the oncoming rider and were interested in him. One of them, the rider on the near side, closest to George, looked like Hank. At least he was thick and burly, but until George was a lot closer he couldn't be sure.

Finally, one of those three men raised a gloved hand in a high salute, and George returned the greeting. He booted his horse over into a lope, gauging the movement so as to intercept the drag-riders at the forest's fringe, and that is how it worked out.

It *was* Hank, back there on the near-side. He stiff-trotted up to George with a quizzical smile and said, "What brought you out here in the heat?"

George did not answer the question. He pointed. "Are those two men the Bowman brothers?"

Hank nodded. "That's them."

George said, "Come with me," and walked his horse on over to Harlan and John Bowman. They halted and sat gazing at him. George did not waste any time, he told the Bowman brothers essentially what he had also told Shep. They sat like stone carvings. The youngest Bowman knew George on sight, from the interlude with the old buckboard five miles up the stageroad north of Shafter. He accepted everything George said, verbatim. It was his older brother, Harlan, who said, "How do you know all this, Mr. Lefton?"

"Stage driver stopped at Santee's restaurant for breakfast this morning and told Charley. Then I came along, and Charley told me. I went out on the east range and told a friend of mine. A friend of Hank's and mine. He rode back to tell those easterly cowmen to call off their drive. Then he's to meet Hank and me up ahead somewhere."

Harlan's brows drew inward and downward. "Why up ahead?"

George looked at Hank first, before answering Bowman. "Because Hank and Shep and I are going on up ahead, Mr. Bowman, and stake B Bar's claim on the meadows before those outsiders get up there."

Harlan Bowman kept looking quizzically

at George. "Why? I mean, we appreciate this, Mr. Lefton, only why should you and Hank and that other feller buy into our trouble?"

"To *prevent* it, that's why," answered George, a trifle impatiently. "To keep there from being any trouble."

Bowman looked at his brother, then looked from Hank back to George. "I guess I don't understand," he murmured.

There was an easy answer and George gave it. "Have you ever seen a real range war? Well; I have, Mr. Bowman. I don't want to see another one. Can you get along without Hank until we meet up at the meadows?"

Harlan nodded. "Yes."

Hank spoke for the first time. "Where *are* those damned meadows?"

Bowman lifted a gloved hand and pointed. "See the tip of Battle Mountain up there, Hank? Well; up ahead where Jim Bates is riding point you'll find a pretty fair old road. Just follow it, and come late afternoon you'll see the meadows at the base of the mountain, and all around it."

George raised his reinhand. "One more thing; when a feller named Shep comes up, tell him where we've gone. All right?"

Harlan nodded soberly. "I'll tell him." He

looked long at George. "We're obliged to you."

George jerked his head and struck out up through the trees. Hank waved to the Bowmans and loped ahead too.

CHAPTER ELEVEN: RIDE TO BATTLE MOUNTAIN

It wasn't rugged terrain. In fact, although there were fir and pine trees most of the way, there was a lot of graze and browse up in the mountains. Unlike the Rockies farther north, New Mexico had some fairly open and hospitable uplands.

The trail Harlan Bowman had mentioned up ahead of the drive was actually an old road. It was badly washed out in places, but sometime, perhaps back during those warring times Charley Santee liked to talk about, someone had carved out a wagon-road. This was what still remained of it.

Hank couldn't imagine why anyone would go to all that work. George said, "Wagon-road for soldiers. You know the army doesn't go anywhere it can't bring along its wheeled vehicles and guns."

Hank said no more.

They found that the old road had a special advantage; it did not head directly for Battle

Mountain, but followed around the sidehills gaining elevation only gradually, which was good engineering. It also happened to be the way four-legged animals, who knew nothing about engineering, also made their trails through mountainous country. Most army roads, in fact, relied less upon engineers and more often upon, old, circuitous, game trails.

When they paused in a warm grassy place to rest and water the horses at a marshy little clear-water spring, Hank built a cigarette, lit it, and looked all around. "Sure pretty up here," he said, then stopped turning as he considered the looming, dark face of Battle Mountain. "You sure Shep'll get up here?"

George was sure. What he wasn't sure about was where those riders coming down from the north might be. "Don't worry about Shep," he answered. "Worry about the strangers."

They struck on across the little park back into more trees, and stayed with the old road until it topped out upon a large meadow with grass stirrup-high to a mounted man. No one needed to tell them they had found the first of the Battle Mountain graze.

From here on, although there were dense

stands of enormous, over-ripe big forest monarchs, there were more wide meadows too, and the land no longer tipped upwards, but began to flatten out a little. There were still cresting places, great, enormous rolls of grassland that ran for miles, but on each side of the crests they only sloped very little, usually down into a brushy or tree-grown gentle swale, then rose up to make more large meadows.

There was water in every swale George and Hank traversed. Finally, at the base of the awesome huge old half-dome-like granite peak, George saw where a large camp had once been. He also saw something else; where a fire had consumed all the trees around this place.

Hank dismounted and took a stick to poke around. He turned up a hexagonal rifle barrel with the stock burnt off. The gun-barrel had survived many icy winters, its hammer frozen forever in a cocked position.

George swung down, related what Charley Santee had told him, and Hank shook his head as he continued to stare at the old gun-barrel.

"Pity," he said. Then he looked up, giving voice to the practical truth as rangemen knew it. "Too damned bad they had to get wiped out; too bad they didn't just high-tail up north where no one would bother them. But then, like my old pappy used to say, everyone has his turn at getting overrun; all you got to do is live long enough and it'll be your turn."

They led their horses across the meadow and saw a small herd of elk, who fled, two golden eagles, who soared, keeping an eye upon the trespassing two-legged creatures, and, with the sun sliding off-centre by a fair distance, decided that the only way they were going to be able to find the invading cowmen from the north was to climb up at least part way, on the mountain, which would give them a view of the north country on the downward side of the uplands.

Hank was not very enthusiastic. As he shed his hat and gunbelt and spurs, he kept squinting upwards. Finally, as George struck off up a wide, stony crevice, Hank said, "You know, if a feller fell off up there, George, his clothes would be out of style before he hit the ground. And I never liked climbing higher'n a saddle anyway. Makes my hands sweat."

But Hank climbed. Grimly, carefully, and silently, but he climbed. George led the way; he was not fond of this undertaking either, but there was no other way, short of riding perhaps eight or ten miles northward, and if they'd done that, darkness would catch them, so he climbed.

They did not have to get all the way to the top, which was fortunate because Battle Mountain was a huge upthrust; just guessing, George thought the top of the thing had to be at least 10,000 feet above sea level, but he did not waste much time thinking about this, once he saw the dust down the far slope. He waited until Hank came up, then pointed.

"The stage driver was right. There they are, just coming up off the range down there."

Hank forgot his dread of heights to look. "They'll camp down there tonight and make the final drive come daylight." He looked elsewhere. It was a breathtaking, magnificent view of the entire countryside, but after one look Hank wiped his palms and turned back. "Let's get the hell back down off of here," he said.

They climbed down, taking longer at this than they had taken climbing upwards. When, eventually, they reached ground, the sun was gone somewhere beyond the westerly rims, but because this was summertime, daylight would not leave for several hours yet.

George was quiet; he had fairly well plotted the lie of the southward landform, and with an idea beginning to form he went out where his horse was grazing without looking elsewhere. Only when Hank called him, did George raise his head. A horseman was coming at a loose jog towards them.

Shep.

George did not mount up, but led his animal over where Hank, looking probably as much relieved to be back upon level ground again, as at seeing Frank Shepherd approaching, fished for his tobacco and papers. "Like old times," he said, without explaining what he'd meant by that.

Shep walked his horse the last couple of hundred yards. "Hey," he called ahead, his coarse features bent into their customary devil-may-care, half-laughing, half-challenging expression. "Them B Bar fellers sure wanted to come with me." He drew rein, stepped down and grinned. "You find them trespassers?"

Hank gestured with his cigarette. "On down the far slope, six, seven miles, maybe less. Looks like a fair-sized drive." Hank dropped his arm. "They'll camp down there tonight and make the big push tomorrow. They could be up here, easy, before B Bar makes it, I think, if they kept on going today."

"Except that they don't know the way," suggested George, "and you can lose a lot of cattle in this kind of country trying to move through forests in the dark."

Shep hitched at his shellbelt, twisted to glance around, then said, "Hell; there's enough feed up in here for half the cattle around the Shafter country. I don't see why just one outfit's got to hold it all."

That may have been right, and it may not have been. George wasn't concerned. "We've got a couple of hours of light left," he told the other two. "If we can get even part way down the south slope in the direction of that drive, we'd ought to be able to pick up their firelight after nightfall, hadn't we?"

Shep came back to thinking in terms of what lay ahead. "I reckon so. What have you in mind?"

"Ride on down there and turn them back," said George. "Two of us will ride in and talk, one of us will lie back and bust the herd back northward if there is trouble."

It was a very elemental plan, but then there did not have to be anything complicated about it, since they would be dealing more with several hundred dumb-brute cattle, more than with the drovers who had brought them this far. Cattle could be stampeded very easily at night, especially in strange country, and especially when that strange country exploded with gunfire, in their faces.

Shep looked at Hank, who shrugged his thick shoulders. "It'll work," he said to the Texan. "Let's go before darkness catches us in the damned trees and we get lost."

George didn't think they could get lost, not so long as they had a campfire down the far slope somewhere to pilot them on in, and he was positive the fire would be a big one; no one drove hundreds of head of cattle without using a number of drovers, and drovers ate like horses, which required a large cooking fire.

He was right, but it was almost three hours, and the gloom of late evening had set in before they saw the campfire, and even then it looked to Shep as though it were miles away, off down through a tangled blackness of trees and underbrush. Shep halted his horse, raised up in the stirrups, looked down there, then said, "Whooee! Them fellers look a hunnert miles away, George, supposing they got dogs with 'em?"

George pushed his horse on down the slope. "Then they'll hear us and bark," he said, pushing onward. "And the riders will thinks it's catamounts or bears." He looked back grinning, "I hope."

Hank laughed and went down next. The last man to head into the night-mantled downslope trees and gloom was Shep. He called ahead. "Hey; let me guess; you two fellers figure to ride in and talk, and I'm the feller who lies back up the slope and stampedes the cattle. Right?"

George smiled to himself. He knew Frank Shepherd. "You and Hank can ride in," he called back. "I'll lie back and bust the herd. All right?"

Shep answered quickly. "Nope. I'll do the busting. George, you're the talker in this outfit. How about that, Hank?"

The answer came back belatedly, and only after Hank swore painfully because he'd failed to duck and a low pine limb had struck him across the forehead nearly making him lose his hat. When he was straight in the saddle again he said, irritably, "Why don't you shut up, Shep?"

They went down into the darkness single file, George out front and Shep farthest back. It wasn't as bad as they had anticipated; there were little meadows and parks on the far side of the mountain, too, but until the moon arose and some stars came to help dispel the gloom, they rode carefully. Mountain-side riding was risky even in broad daylight, but after sunset it was downright perilous.

No one spoke again until, much later, they could all pick up the tantalising scent of meat cooking. By then they had a sighting to head on in on. The campfire was big, and it was at the fringe of the forest. Out beyond were the cattle, bedded down now, and willing to be quiet. They had been walking most of the day, grabbing grass as they meandered along, so they probably weren't very hungry, but it was a cinch they were tired.

Finally, when the firelight was brightest on ahead no more than two hundred yards, George halted in the pitchblende tree-gloom. When Hank and Shep rode up beside him, he looked at the Texan and Shep looked back. "Meet back here?" he asked, and as George nodded, Shep reined out and around heading for the rangeland beyond the trees where the cattle were. George did not worry; Shep was like an Indian when he wanted to be.

He jerked his head. Hank kept even with him as they rode the last couple of hundred yards down into the firelight.

CHAPTER TWELVE:
A FACE-DOWN

If there were dogs with the drovers they neither barked nor charged up as a pair of ghostly riders came forth into the farthest firelight and were first seen by a young cowboy who sprang up so fast he upset his tin of coffee.

Several others also arose, all young, all hard-faced in the jumping, orange firelight. There were seven men that George saw, and he guessed there might be a man or two out with the cattle, nighthawking, and there would also more than likely be another man or two somewhere else beyond the firelight. It looked like a fairly large riding-crew for no more than four or five hundred head of cattle.

Not all the riders were young. The man who had been using his saddle as though it were a chair, on across the fire, was stocky and grizzled and grey. There were several other older riders, perhaps not as old as the man sitting on his saddle over there, watching as George and Hank picked their way forward, but definitely older than that spooky young buckaroo back nearer the forest who'd jumped up so fast he'd spilt his coffee.

Those older riders did not jump up. In fact they did not move at all. They sat, plates balanced on their folded legs, watching as George and Hank swung off and, trailing their horses by the reins, walked around where the grey man sat. The grey man put aside his meal and got up a little stiffly. His face was craggy in any case, but right now it was granite-set. No one spoke until this man said, "You boys could damned easy get shot, slipping up on a drover's camp like you did."

George halted ten feet off, counted the crew, studied several of the older, rougher-looking riders, then ignored the greying man's remonstrance to say, "Mind if I ask where you're taking this herd, mister?"

The greying man had been studying his two visitors. He said, "No, I expect I don't mind. We're taking them to the meadows up around Battle Mountain."

Hank settled his weight on one leg, hooked his thumbs and studied the riders as though the greying man did not exist. This was George's palaver as far as Hank was concerned, and those tough-eyed squatting men were Hank's concern.

"There are cattle up on the Battle Mountain meadows already," said George. "That's drought-range for the cowmen over around Shafter."

A lanky, rawboned squatting man with his soiled and stained black hat pushed far back spoke up. "Naw, mister, there ain't no cattle on them meadows. I scouted them meadows early this morning. There ain't nothing up there."

Hank gazed at this man. "You're a lousy scout," he said quietly. "You should have gone across and looked down the far side. The herd was moving up from B Bar range. Mister, I was with it."

The greying man looked at Hank, then at his cowboy, then back to George. "How many cattle are up there?" he asked.

George took a long guess. He had seen B Bar's drive but hadn't asked for a tally. "Three-fifty, four hundred head."

"When did they get up there?"

"Late this afternoon," replied George. "That isn't free-graze anyway, mister."

The greying man studied George thoughtfully, then he said, "As far as I'm concerned it is. My name's Arch Colton. I run a couple thousand head over on the Inferno rancheria. It's going dry awful fast over there, so I scouted up this country and found those meadows with no stock on them."

"There's stock on them now, Mr. Colton," stated George.

All the riders, hunkering around their fire, had put aside their tin plates and were sitting as motionless as stone images, looking and listening. George Lefton and Arch Colton were finally at the crux of this meeting.

Colton said, "That's big country up there, cowboy. Plenty of room. By the way, what's your name?"

"George Lefton. This here is Hank Burton."

Colton was momentarily silent, as though groping for his future course, then he said, "Well, boys, we're coming on up, so you'd better go tell your boss if he's got any unmarked critters he'd better get 'em branded before tomorrow, otherwise they might drift in with my animals and get marked with our brand by mistake."

George felt the atmosphere changing but did not take his eyes off the greying, hard-faced cowman. "You're not going up," he said, softly.

Colton's craggy features slowly changed, slowly showed force and cruelty. "Cowboy, if you're the smartest rider your boss has, he's got to be riding with an awful stupid bunch; a couple of fellers don't stand a chance, riding into a Colton camp like you two did. You'd better go back while you're still able to ride, and tell your boss Arch

Colton's coming, and he don't hire just ordinary rangeriders."

George took this threat without blinking. "You've got three choices, Mr. Colton. As I see it, you can start something with Hank and me — and get killed right where you're standing, regardless of what happens to Hank and me, or you can saddle up come dawn and head back the way you came, or you can fire one shot, any one of you, and signal our friends out yonder waiting for such a signal, and they'll stampede your herd in ten different directions so's it'll take you a month to round them up again."

Arch Colton did not turn, but all the sitting men around the campfire began moving a little, began twisting to peer out into the night around them, and southward out where the bedded herd lay.

Colton was quiet for at least ten seconds, never taking his eyes off George Lefton. Then, he slowly wagged his head. "That's a lousy bluff, cowboy," he said scornfully. "If there'd been more of you my nighthawks out with the herd would have known it and raised the yell by now."

"No bluff at all," George replied. He dropped his right hand to let it lie atop the saw-handle of his sixgun. "Want me to fire one shot so you can see whether it's a bluff or not?"

Colton's expression turned savage. He had been called. "You take your hand off the gun, cowboy, or you're going to get yourself killed."

George did not move the hand. "I'll promise you one thing, Mr. Colton, you won't see it happen. You'll be heading on out before I do."

The raw-boned rider with the tipped-back black hat said, "Mr. Colton, get him to call them other fellers in. That'll prove whether they're out there or not. And maybe we could set down and talk this over."

Hank, who had already singled this man out, snarled at him, "Shut up, you! Don't try and be foxy, because no one's going to come in so's you fellers can get the drop on them."

The rawboned man stiffened. He was Colton's range-boss. He could not submit to being told to shut up in front of the other riders. Very slowly, without taking his eyes off Hank, he unwound up off the ground. "Mister," he said gently, "you just bought yourself a headstone."

George scarcely moved but when Colton looked, a blue-black gunmuzzle was looking back. "Tell your banty rooster to sit down," George said, and eased back the hammer, a sound that carried easily to every seated man.

Colton raised his eyes to George's face. He could not take the chance; he did not know the man who had made that sudden, blinding-flash draw, but he was sure of one thing, anyone who could draw like that, *would* shoot.

"Sit down, Jeff," he exclaimed.

The rawboned man, and the other Colton riders, were motionless, all but their eyes. They too had seen that draw. Jeff sat down, keeping both hands well in sight as he did so. Hank rubbed it in a little by grinning.

George did not leather his sixgun. "What'll it be, Mr. Colton; a fight, a stampede, or a pull-out in the morning?"

There was no choice even though it had sounded as though there might be. Colton drew down a breath, then gently let it out. If there was no one down there ready to stampede his herd, and his riders found this out, the story of Arch Colton being bluffed by a pair of cowboys carrying ivory-handled sixguns, when all his riding crew was sitting there ready to kill the interlopers, would spread until Arch Colton would be the laughing-stock of the New Mexico range country, which was something no big cowman could stand in a land where nerve and courage and shrewdness were all that kept a man on top.

On the other hand, he had seen that cowboy draw; he was satisfied about one thing, maybe George Lefton was someone's rider *now,* but Arch Colton, who had been hiring tough, seasoned rangemen all his life, knew for a fact that anyone who could draw a gun like that hadn't always been a cowboy, or, if he had, he'd certainly been a very unusual and deadly one, so Colton's choice was no choice at all. He turned back facing the fire, convinced that George would shoot. Losing face was bad, but being dead was a hell of a lot worse.

"There's some free-graze west of here about sixty miles," he grumbled, and sat down upon his saddle and reached to pick up his tin plate where he'd set it aside.

He did not look up again.

George and Hank hung there a moment longer, waiting, but this seemed to be the end of it, so George nodded and Hank walked away, out into the darkness beyond the firelight. Then he drew his gun, cocked it so that everyone around the fire knew what he was doing, then, finally, George also walked out into the night. No one at the campfire moved, but the rawboned rider turned, eventually, after about ten minutes had passed, and craned around. When he turned back Arch Colton was bitterly eyeing the yonder night.

"You want to make fifty dollars?" he asked the range-boss.

Three other men put aside their plates too, and also arose when the rawboned man called Jeff arose, smiling. Jeff said, "I'd almost do this for nothin', Mr. Colton." He looked at the other three and jerked his head.

Several of the other riders would have also arisen to go off with Jeff and his friends towards the rope corral where their horses were, but Colton shook his head.

"No need, boys. I'll want the rest of you to head the herd away from here anyway. We don't want to be nowhere around when they kill those two. As far as I know there's no law anywhere around here, but all the same we won't take the chance."

The disappointed men sank back down. The meal was over. Not much was said among the riders at the fire as they refilled their tin cups with coffee and most of them built smokes and settled back to get comfortable, until an older cowboy, looking pensive, said, "Mr. Colton, sixty miles further west is a hell of a drive. Jeff said them meadows up by that big peak are only about six, seven miles. We're going to have some footsore critters if we go the long way."

Colton did not dispute this, but he was a cowman and he thought as one when he said, "Spence, maybe that cowboy would have pulled the trigger, I don't know. But I *do* know that if there is already a big herd up on those meadows and we pushed on up there with our herd, the grass would be gone in a month or two, and we'd still have to move them out again to new free-graze, and by then it'd all be took up. It's not the ride that decided me, it's the amount of grass." Colton drained his tin cup, then smiled wintrily. "The damned gun wasn't what made up my mind. I've looked into my share of them before. What we're worrying about is *grass.* You understand?"

Evidently the cowboy did because he grunted, took a long pull on his cigarette, then lay back, head upon his saddle-seat, and tipped down his hat to shield his eyes from fireglow.

Colton had called it exactly as he had analysed it. The sending of those four men out to kill George and Hank had, for a man as hard and practical and ruthless as Arch Colton, been a sort of off-hand gesture of retaliation. He was already thinking past this event because, as he'd explained, grass, not men, were important to a cow outfit in a drought season.

He got his cup refilled, built a smoke, hunkered in the flickering light, and when the nighthawk rode in to report that the herd was quiet, Arch Colton looked searchingly at the man, but said nothing. The nighthawk obviously hadn't seen anything or he'd have reported it; he probably wouldn't have seen it anyway, because if there were more of those men from Battle Mountain out there, they would make a particular point of not being seen. In the morning, Colton thought, if there *had* been anyone, he and his men would find their tracks. He hoped there *had* been. No man liked to be made to look bad, particularly in front of other men.

CHAPTER THIRTEEN: AMBUSHED!

Shep had to function by guess and by damn. He knew George had probably brought it off when more than a half hour had elapsed and there was no shooting, but he did *not* have any way of knowing when George and Hank left the cowcamp, so he lingered out there, just beyond sight of Colton's nighthawks, and finally decided to head for the previously arranged rendezvous only when one of the nighthawks rode in to be relieved.

He was fairly certain that by this time George and Hank had pulled out, but just to make certain he trailed the nighthawk back in the direction of the cowcamp hoping to catch a glimpse of someone, either those ornery trespassers or his pardners.

What Shep saw, from out in the deep darkness, were several riders walking their horses into the forest northwest of the cowcamp, and being very quiet about it.

Shep lifted his hat, scratched his head over this, resettled his hat and told his horse that those four men ought to be ashamed of themselves, doing what it looked like they were up to. Then Shep headed off in the same northwesterly direction; he never did get back to the rendezvous in time to meet George or Hank. He could have, because the other two men waited up there for a while then headed on back up the slope for Battle Mountain, confident Shep would join them on the trail somewhere. The reason Shep didn't try to meet them at the rendezvous was elemental; he couldn't, those other four horsemen were between him and where he was supposed to meet his friends.

George and Hank did not worry. As Hank

said, "There hasn't been a common rangerider born who could catch Shep if he didn't want to be caught."

George had no comment. They had a long way to travel and through the darkness at that. He was not at all satisfied Colton wouldn't want him dead, but he had doubts about Colton being able to find him up the mountainside in daylight, since Colton and his men were not familiar with the terrain, let alone at night. In fact, as the darkness deepened through the forests they had to traverse, George was not altogether satisfied he and Hank wouldn't also end up lost.

But that really did not matter as long as they continued to travel in the correct general direction. They had no appointment to meet anyone up ahead, and even if they yawed a little east or west, come daylight they could correct it and still reach Battle Mountain meadows to juncture with B Bar.

Once, some coursing wolves sounded in full throat. They had probably startled a deer or an elk out of its bed and were chasing it along the slope. And again, a half hour later, they heard a catamount wail. This time their horses got right up in the bit, frightened half to death even though the panther did not sound very close. Nor would he try to get any closer, for although he had a sweet-tooth for horsemeat and cowmeat, those two enticing aromas were now also mingled with the smell of men, and there wasn't a cougar living who didn't leave the country after just one faint whiff of man-smell.

Hank called for a halt, when they reached a grassy benchland with moonlight making the trees look ghostly, stepped down and snugged up his cincha. Then he straightened up a little, leaned upon the horse peering back southward. He said, "Did you hear anything, George?"

They both listened for a full minute, then George turned to ride on. "Probably Shep," he said, and led the way on across the benchland and into another stand of trees.

Hank developed rearward anxiety after this and turned to look and listen a number of times before they finally halted to blow the horses about a mile or a mile and a half from the top-out.

There was a clearing, man-made evidently because in the side of an almost perpendicular rock facing at the far side of the clearing was an eerie black cave where some early-day prospector had tried to trace a gold ledge back to its source.

If there had ever been a cabin or a lean-to in this ghostly, quiet place it had long since turned to dust, as had the miner who had chiselled away so patiently into that rock face, no doubt. A small creek came around one side of the rock face and pooled where rocks had been fitted with infinite patience to make a place large enough for a man to bathe and do his laundry. The sound of this water trilling over worn stones obscured most other sounds, by the time George and Hank got over there, but the sound diminished almost entirely when they walked farther, leading their horses, and peered curiously into the mine.

Hank was impressed; even by starshine it was easy to see that the mine had been hacked through living stone, mostly quartz or granite. "That feller sure must have hated rocks," said Hank, craning inside. "I wonder how deep he went?"

George grinned. "I'll hold your horse; go on in and have a look."

Hank recoiled. "The hell I will. There could be a whole passel of panthers in there or maybe a denned-up old sow-bear." Hank turned and walked back to the pool, let his horse drag the reins, grazing, while Hank dropped belly-down to fill up with cold water.

George, also allowing his horse time to pick grass and rest, turned back from the mine also. He had the rock face at his back, its layers of gloom covering everything but the paleness of his face.

It was possible to dimly and distantly make out the northward range country from this elevation, but not much else, and even the range country appeared only as an indistinct, tawny-tan great expanse. Visibility was no better up close, either, not entirely because there wasn't much of a moon, but because even the starshine could not make much of an impression where such thick, massive stands of timber cast great shadows.

George started to turn, to also go over and tank up at the little pool. His horse had ambled over to be closer to Hank's horse. George was by himself when he turned, so, when the explosion came and the bullet flattened with a vicious, splattering suddenness against the rock face, it had missed George's head by about eight inches.

He reacted by instinct, dropped low, moved sideways, drew and swung his weapon, but he had not seen the muzzleblast. It was gone before he got completely squared around.

Hank called out. "George? You all right?"

George only answered after he had begun moving, fading back towards the layers of darkness in front of the rock face, but sliding along eastward in Hank's direction.

"Yeah, I'm all right," he said, straining for a sighting down through the yonder trees where the assassin had to be. "If he can't shoot any straighter than that, I'm not worried."

Obviously, since the night was utterly still now, George's retort had gone at least as far as the gunman. Another gunshot erupted, but this time both of the men near the rock face were watching and ready. They fired back almost simultaneously, aiming at the muzzleblast, but George at least had no high hopes. There were too many old giant trees down where that man had fired from, and of course he would have fired from behind one of them.

But those two shots from near the pool must have inspired some respect in someone, because there was no more firing from down the south slope for a long while.

George got over by the pool. Hank had nipped around where the water was trickling down, and had got close to several pine trees. When George came close he lowered his voice and said, "I *knew* I heard something back there a couple of miles. I knew damned well I did. That greyheaded old bastard down there in his cowcamp sent someone up to even the score with us."

George stepped close to a tree, shucked out his spent casing, dropped in a fresh load from a belt loop, then quietly said, "The question is, Hank, how *many* did he send after us?"

Without any warning a gunshot split the silence from eastward, which was where the trail to the little mine-meadow lay, and that of course meant that George and Hank were bottled up, unless there was a trail out to the west.

Maybe there was, but they never saw it. Another gunman opened up from that direction, only this man fired twice, very fast, then, after about a five second pause, he let fly again with a third shot. He was clearly trying to ground-sluice with lead in an off-chance that he might hit either George or Hank.

Hank would have fired back but George reached and pushed his hand down. "The minute you do, that feller southward will see the flash. That's their idea — bait us, then bracket wherever we're shooting from." George leaned upon his tree. "I think there's four or five of them."

Hank hadn't counted. "It's nice odds whatever they are," he said dryly. "The last time I had to face odds of two-to-one was the day I rode another kid's danged horse home from school, and when he come after it, he brought along his four brothers. You know, I never got such a whipping since."

George smiled. Hank, cranky though he undeniably was at times, and as much of a worrier as he also was, did not know the meaning of the word fear.

Hank stepped from behind a tree and peered. "Well; what do we do now, stand here like crows on a limb and wait until daylight so they can pick us off?"

George did not answer. Something was moving down the slope to the southward. It sounded like a horseman withdrawing back down the hill, but it did not necessarily have to be any such thing at all. "Wait," he said. "Just wait."

That quick-triggered gunman to the west suddenly repeated his earlier ground-sluicing tactic again, only this time he fired four times. Three times very fast, then he paused, and let fly his fourth shot. George figured out how the man did that. He raked the area with those three shots, then listened intently for movement, and fired his last round as a sound-shot. The trouble was, he couldn't have heard anything because neither George nor Hank had to move.

The moment that last shot came and

went, the gunman eastward, who was evidently guarding the trail, let fly with one round, and from down the slope either one man fired two fast shots, or two men fired one shot each, George could not tell which it was, and he did not really try very hard to make it out. He had an idea.

"Stay put," he told Hank. "Watch the horses and stay where you are."

Hank stepped forth to protest as George began a crouching advance along the black stone face, westerly, but he had waited a moment too long, or George had moved away too quickly, so Hank hung there, squinting his eyes nearly closed watching George's progress. He could only see George as far as the mine-shaft. Beyond, it was simply too dark.

That was what George was counting on. In fact he was betting his life on the darkness as he continued to stealthily approach the area beyond the mine, beyond the grassy little meadow, where the trigger-happy gunman was holed-up among some huge fir trees.

His entire concentration was focused ahead where the darkness formed a continuum beyond the stone face into the trees. If the gunman out there saw *him* before *he* saw the gunman . . .

He paused, listened, then re-gripped his cocked weapon and resumed the stalk. The biggest danger was the one that eventually brought this personal duel to a flaming conclusion; George stepped into a pile of loose shale. The noise was like breaking egg shells. He reacted immediately by throwing himself sidewards and downward. The gunshot came, a blinding flash of red. George heard the lead splatter against rock over where he had been when he'd rattled the shale. He pulled off his hat, shoved it over the muzzle of his sixgun, and when the second shot flashed, he drove a bullet directly into it.

There was no third shot. Silence filled in the night after the death of the last fading echo. George looked down. He had effectively smothered his own muzzle-blast so that that man down the slope could not shoot at him with any accuracy. He had also shot the entire crown out of his hat.

Without any warning a flurry of fierce gunshots erupted down the south slope and a man cried out in a startled, frightened voice. As suddenly as this firing had erupted it also ended. Then George heard a familiar voice sing out.

"Hey, you crazy bastard, you better drop that carbine or the next one'll bust your lousy spine!"

George rolled clear and began re-loading. He smiled in the grass. Shep had finally caught up with them.

Chapter Fourteen: Back to Battle Mountain

They could hear someone over eastward heading back down the slope astride a hurrying horse. George got back where Hank was, about the time someone down the slope let out a squawk, but there was no gunfire. Hank was worried, but then Hank always started to worry when he couldn't see trouble or didn't understand what might be going on around him.

"That's Shep down there," he hissed as George returned. "We got to go over there and help him."

George held out a restraining arm. "Stay here. That was Shep who bellered, and that's all we've got to know."

"But if we don't —"

"Hank, damn it all, you go over there and bust down through those trees and if Colton's man doesn't shoot you, Shep will."

Hank subsided. They stood together in the darkness and waited. It seemed an interminable length of time before a voice called ahead as three mounted men appeared, ghost-like, over upon the south edge of the little mine-meadow.

"Hey, fellers, this is Shep. I got me a couple of bushwhackers. Now don't limber up or you might shoot me. Where'n hell are you?"

George wanted to laugh. "Over on the east side," he called back, and watched the three riders turn in his direction.

Hank blew out a big, relieved, ragged sigh. "Darn fool, trying to take them alive," he muttered, but when Shep came over and stepped to earth Hank was the first one out there.

"You all right?" he asked, and Shep's raffish smile was as good an answer as any.

"Yeah, I'm all right, but the boy up there on the bay horse has got a busted arm. You know, night-shootin' ain't too good in a forest; I was trying for his gunhand. Missed by ten inches."

George walked ahead, recognised the two captives, one hunched across his saddlehorn in pain, as some of the rangemen from Colton's camp. He told them to dismount. As they did so, he said, "Go over 'em, Hank. I'm curious about that ground-sluicing feller over in the trees yonder." George

146

started over there, and even though he was confident there would be no more gunfire, he nonetheless kept close to the stone face until he got among the trees.

He found his adversary flat out. It was the man who had offered to fight Hank, the one Colton called Jeff. He had caught George's slug plumb centre.

George went further back, found the man's horse, brought it in, boosted the body across the saddle, lashed it in place, then led the horse back over where Hank and Shep were supervising the bandaging of the injured rider's broken arm. No one said a word as George led up the horse with the belly-down rider tied across it. They all looked up, but no one said anything until the bandaging was finished.

Shep looked at the man whose arm he had broken. "You know, mister, you're lucky. I been behind the four of you most of the way up the slope. I guess I should have dusted you out of your saddle back a couple of miles, only I didn't like the odds too much, in among them damned trees."

Hank went over, looked at the dead man, came back and shook his head. "I figured he was mostly talk, back there at the cow-camp."

Shep pointed to the uninjured cowboy.

"He was trying to hightail it downhill from over to the east." Shep turned to George. "Well; if we take them on back to B Bar, they'll just hang 'em, so why don't we do it right here and save everyone the trouble."

The uninjured rider looked up. He was young. He was also as white as a sheet. "Listen, Mr. Colton's taking the herd on west come sunup. We're leaving this country for good and all. Don't that entitle me and Mac to go back? You beat us. You even beat Mr. Colton. Ain't that enough?"

George thought it was. He motioned. "Help your friend up, then get on your horse," he commanded, and the uninjured rider did not waste a moment in obeying. George looked at Hank. "Give him the reins," he said, and Hank handed them up.

Shep made a clucking sound and wagged his head. "George; someday being lenient's goin' to get you killed." But otherwise Shep offered no objection when George jerked his head for the riders to head on down the mountain. Afterwards, Shep pulled out a tobacco sack and made a smoke. The episode was finished as far as he was concerned. If he, instead of George, had killed that man over in the westerly trees, Shep still would have acted the same.

He turned towards his horse. "Well; it

148

can't be much farther to the meadows," he said, and stepped across the saddle eyeing the uphill slope. "I think I can see the top-off up there."

George let Shep take the lead as they left the mine-meadow, heading back eastward to the trail. This time as they rode, George brought up the rear. He did not feel especially bad about killing Colton's rangeboss; he just did not feel very good about killing *anyone.*

They rode steadily for a solid hour. It took that long in the darkness to climb up a mile or a mile and half whereas if they had been on level, unobstructed ground, they could have covered five or six times that distance in the same period of time.

The horses were in fair shape, although Shep's animal hadn't had as much rest as the other two when they finally reached the meadows, so he was willing to slacken pace as the three of them came together, with Battle Mountain's gigantic peak lofting upwards dead ahead several miles.

Shep pointed: "That way." George and Hank did not argue. As they walked out level, for a change, Hank said, "I wouldn't put it past that damned old cuss down there to head up here with his whole crew, to get even."

George doubted that Colton would do that. He doubted it very much.

Shep said, "All I'm worryin' about right now is something to eat. Do you boys know that I could eat a buffler commencin' at the rear, if someone would hold his head?"

The night had begun to turn slightly chilly. George had no idea what time it was, but judging from the cast of the lopsided moon it had to be past midnight; perhaps even one or two o'clock in the morning. He yawned, kept the peak on his right, and rode along until the cold compelled him to reach back, unlash his jumper, and put it on. Shep and Hank did the same.

It was Hank who first lifted his head, sniffing. "Cattle," he announced. "You fellers smell them?"

No one answered because no one smelled cattle, but another mile or so onward George detected the scent. He also detected an even more welcome smell; woodsmoke. B Bar would be bedded down, but as long as there was some food left, and some embers to be stirred to fresh light, B Bar could sleep right on through until daybreak for all he cared.

They found the camp without much difficulty, and they also were found by one of Harlan Bowman's two hired riders; it was the older cowboy, Tim Brophy, who had been watching their approach from back in among some aspens, and who finally rode out to intercept them a half mile from camp. When he recognised Hank, he said, "How'd you boys make out; I could have sworn I heard gunshots one hell of a long way off an hour or two back."

George said, "You probably did." That was all he said, though, until, with Brophy falling in to head for camp with them even though he was supposed to be nighthawking the cattle, Hank, who had become friendly with all the B Bar men, gave a curt account of all that had happened.

Brophy did not act the least bit surprised about either the fact that the trespassing herd had been turned back, or that in the gunfight down the far slope, these three, with their ivory-butted guns, had come back unmarked, while some of the trespassers had been shot up. Brophy had made up his mind about those three long ago.

At the camp, George, Hank and Shep cared for their animals first, then turned them loose and went over to see what they could rustle in the way of a meal. Brophy hung around long enough to have a cup of coffee, then he rode back out to do his nighthawking.

Harlan Bowman, a light sleeper evidently, reared up and watched the three, silent, hunkering armed men squatting over by the replenished fire eating ravenously. He rolled out, pulled on his boots, reached for his jacket — he already had his shirt and trousers on — and arose to walk over.

As he knelt and reached for a tin cup he said, "Trouble?"

Hank answered. "One killed, one shot, one captured. All of them sent back down. The feller's name is Arch Colton. He has maybe five, six hundred head. At first he made war-talk, but I guess he'll be trailing over west, about sixty miles now." Hank looked around. Shep nor George had anything to add. They ate and did not even heed Harlan Bowman until he said, "I don't know exactly how to go about this . . ." George and Shep looked up. Bowman smiled a little. "B Bar owes you fellers something. I'd like to make it right with you." Bowman looked from one man to the other. "Any suggestions?"

George picked up his empty coffee cup and held it out. "You're closer to the pot than I am," he said. "You can re-fill this if you will."

Bowman refilled that cup, then, when Shep and Hank held out their cups he also

152

refilled them. As George pulled pulled back he said, "All right, Mr. Bowman. You've paid us." Then he went back to eating. He hadn't really been conscious of his hunger until he'd got close to the camp, then it hit him like a fever.

Harlan Bowman squatted over across the fire studying the three men, one of whom worked for him. He seemed to want to say something, but was hesitant about saying it, or didn't know how to phrase it.

George saw his expression over the firelight and smiled a little. "What chance do you figure a saddle and harness shop would have in Shafter, Mr. Bowman?"

Bowman blinked. He had probably been expecting just about anything under the sun, but this question. "A saddle and harness works . . . ?"

"Yeah. I've been thinking about opening one in town," George explained. "I'm no great shakes as a saddlemaker, but that'll come, and in the meanwhile I'm a pretty fair hand at laying out new harness and mending old harness. What do you think my chances might be?"

Bowman thought for a moment, then said, "Well; for a fact Shafter sure needs a shop like that. I can sure show you a lot of harness rooms on the ranches around here that've been piling up busted stuff for forty years . . . I think it'd succeed."

George slowed down as his appetite was gratified, and eventually sat cross-legged amidst the stars, the slight chill, and the scattering of sleeping men around the fire, and finished his third cup of coffee. He looked at Hank. "You going to stay up here?"

Hank nodded.

George looked at Shep, who flung the grounds from his tin cup into the fire and shook his head. "If you're heading on back, I'll ride with you."

They arose. Harlan Bowman and Hank went out with them where the horses were drowsing. Bowman pointed to a pair of stocky brown animals. "Leave yours to rest up and take those, if you like. I'll send Hank along in the morning with your animals."

They shook hands, then George and Shep caught the fresh horses, rigged out and stepped aboard. Bowman and Hank were strolling back to the fire in quiet conversation when Shep's horse, perhaps resentful of the cold blanket, or just feeling sassy, fired. Shep let out a squawk and tried to regain his balance. He rode the horse out; but he wouldn't have been able to if the horse had really bucked, because Shep was caught completely off guard. As the horse sped past, Shep turned and shook a gloved fist toward Harlan Bowman and Hank. "Thanks a whole bunch, damn you," he sang out, then was borne southward and George took out after him laughing. The two men standing back by the fire doubled over laughing.

Harlan Bowman peered down the night where Shep and George had disappeared and gasped for breath as he said, "I plumb forgot. That's the one that bucks."

George did not overtake Shep until they were near the drop off that headed down towards the Shafter country. By then Shep had his horse ridden down. After that one explosion, the husky little horse went along as though he had been Shep's pet all his life, but Shep never quite took an eye off the little ears in front of him.

"That's gratitude," he complained to George, as they started down the far slope in the early, cold morning. "You do a feller a favour, and what's he do for you; try to get you killed on a damned horse!"

George tried to hold it back, but the laughter came anyway. Shep eyed his partner for a while, then he too laughed.

Chapter Fifteen:
An End To Something

Shep might ordinarily have split off above town and ridden on eastward to one of the bunkhouses where he had been welcome for the past month or so, but town was closer, he said, it was getting damned cold to be riding when you didn't have to, and he didn't have anything to tell the men on the east range that wouldn't be just as fresh in daylight, so he rode on down to the liverybarn, put up his horse, exactly as George also did, saw that the animal was cuffed down, grained, stalled and hayed, then Shep shook off George's offer of part of his room and climbed up into the hayloft to sleep, while George walked up the empty roadway to his room over the gunshop.

It was much closer to getting-up time than to bedding-down time when George took a last long look out his roadway window, then rolled in, and he slept like a log, too. What awakened him was a freight outfit grinding down through the centre of town, but he probably was ready to awaken anyway.

He dressed, then went down to the washroom, shaved and made himself respectable, and hiked diagonally across the road to Charley Santee's place for something to eat.

Shep was already over there, smoking, drinking coffee, and looking pleasantly refreshed. He looked around when George came in, and Charley Santee went shuffling off to fry up some spuds with broken-yolked eggs mixed in. Charley called over his greeting. George answered, then, when Charley brought some coffee before going back to his cooking, Shep pushed out his cigarette and said, "Today's my last day. I'll stop by and pick up my old Texas running-mate, then head on out. I got to thinking about it this morning. I'd like to stick around and see you open your harness shop, but hell, you'll do just fine, and if I keep putting this off, the ranch down in Texas might be gone by the time I get down there." Shep looked steadily at George a moment. "I don't figure a man gets too many chances in this lifetime, and I don't figure he'd ought to put off takin' advantage of 'em. Do you?"

George drank a little coffee before answering. "Probably not," he mused aloud. "Be damned careful, Shep."

The Texan nodded. "Yeah. By the way, I picked up a newspaper in the liverybarn this morning." Shep reached under his jacket and handed it over. The paper was old and slightly torn, and worn thin from handling. Shep's big thumb landed upon an article that told of a daring bank robbery up in Laramie, Wyoming. George read a couple of paragraphs before Shep tapped a paragraph near the bottom of the column. "Read that," he said. "The rest of it just gives a sort of poor description of the three fellers who robbed the bank, and how they disappeared into thin air afterwards, which we know, but read *that* paragraph."

George obeyed. The money they had taken, said the article, one hundred and fifty thousand dollars, had been brought and deposited by the Wyoming Stock Growers Association, part of the Association's warchest to be used in prosecuting their war against homesteaders, sheepmen, and other troublesome people.

George re-read the paragraph, then lifted the paper as Charley brought his breakfast to read it for the third time. When he carefully folded the paper Shep was looking at him with a quizzical grin. After Charley had gone to get the coffee pot to refill their cups, Shep said, "Now, it never bothered my conscience none, George, but I always figured it was bothering you a little and maybe it would get to troublin' Hank a little too. Keep that paper. Give it to Hank when he brings our horses down this morning. Then you fellers remember something we was told up there in Wyoming about that Stock Growers' Association; they was going to hire professional gunfighters to wipe out those settlers." Shep went silent when Charley returned, smiling and talkative.

George ate, listened, mostly, while Charley did all the talking, and did some private speculating. When breakfast was over he and Shep drifted outside. George had the old newspaper in his pocket. Shep stood out there in the rising, dry heat of morning and made a cigarette, which he lit looking at George with that same sardonic expression he'd shown back inside the restaurant.

"I'll tell you what that means to me, pardner," he said quietly. "Them Wyoming cattlemen will hire gunmen to try and find us, and that's a heap more dangerous than having lawmen do it. That's the main reason why I decided to head on out, and put still more miles between me'n them. I don't figure they'll ever do it, find us I mean, but all the same I'll feel a heap better in Texas than I'll feel around here, and anyway, I don't belong here. You'n Hank *do* belong here. He'll wind up as foreman or rangeboss for B Bar sure as I'm a foot tall, and you'll end up with a wife and kids and a good harness and saddle business. Me — I'll hire on some Texas boys on my ranch in

Texas, and them damned Wyoming cowmen'll probably dig up another hunnert and fifty thousand, and make their war on the settlers and sheepmen — but by gawd we sure slowed 'em down a mite, didn't we? And I sort of figure by the time they get their warchest built up again, there'll be more settlers and sheepmen than cowmen, so maybe we done the country a service, making off with that money."

George laughed. "You must have stayed awake pretty late last night, Shep."

The raffish Texan smiled. "Not last night, pardner, this morning after I seen that there newspaper. I sat a spell and did some figuring."

Up the road a man sang out. Hank came trotting stiff-legged down through the building heat leading two horses and riding one. When he reined over he leaned and said, "I hope you fellers are satisfied. I had to get up an hour after I bedded down, to reach town this early." He looked over at the liverybarn. "Are the B Bar horses yonder?"

George and Shep stepped down into the roadway dust to walk over to the barn with Hank. They handed their private horses over to the day-man with strict orders for rubdowns, grain and hay, then they took Hank out back where George handed him the

160

newspaper. As soon as Hank saw the paper his expression turned troubled and wary. Without even opening it he said, "I always figured it'd filter down here someday, I mean the news about Laramie."

"Just read it," urged George, and stepped to the barn doorway to see where the hostler was. The man was dutifully cuffing George's chestnut and Shep's thoroughbred horse. There was no one else around. George went back.

Hank was standing there with a furrowed brow, looking a little incredulous. Shep was telling Hank the same thing he had told George. Hank was listening intently. As George walked up he shot him a look.

"Those descriptions are lousy," he said, when Shep finished speaking. "Hell; those witnesses described just about any three riders in the whole damned country — except for the ivory-butted sixguns."

George nodded. "Shep's pulling out for Texas today, that takes one ivory-handled gun away. Me, a man working in a saddle and harness shop has no need to wear a gun. That leaves you, and what the hell; there are plenty of ivory-handled Colts around, Hank. One man wearing such a gun doesn't prove anything."

Hank thought a moment, then said, "But

161

folks will remember."

George shrugged. "Sure. But if some lawman ever got down here to the Battle Mountain country, which is about as likely as snow in July, how's he going to identify us? By those descriptions of three average-looking cowboys, average height, youngish, with faces covered by bandanas?" George shook his head. "Like I told you before we ever went up there — the only way they'd ever find us would be if we got caught sooner or later raiding another bank. And that is something we won't ever do again. We agreed on that, didn't we?"

Hank, the worrier, let his face clear a little at a time. He glanced once again at the newspaper, then handed it back. George pocketed it. He would burn it the first chance he got. There could be another one, of course, somewhere around town, but the one thing that could arouse some local wonder hadn't been mentioned at all in that article. Perhaps those petrified tellers up at that Laramie bank hadn't noticed it; perhaps the robbery had gone off too smoothly — which it had; after all the three robbers had practised it beforehand until they had it down pat. Nothing was said in the newspaper write-up about all three of those outlaws having ivory-stocked sixguns. That was the best clue, in fact it was the *only* clue, and obviously no one had noticed it.

Hank made a cigarette as he and his two friends stood out back in the shade. They did not push him; Hank was a man who tended to look for the worst in situations. Both George and Shep understood this and did absolutely nothing to push him towards any kind of conclusion.

After a while he looked at them both and smiled a little. "This is the end of it then," he said, looking longest at Shep. "We end up out back of a cowtown liverybarn going our separate ways, eh?"

The other two still said nothing.

Hank blew smoke. "Hell; by right fellers ought to say good-bye over a drink in a saloon, hadn't they?"

Shep smiled. "Naw. Personally, I like the smell down here better'n the smell up there at the Oxbow." He held out a hand to Hank. "If you're ever down Texas-way, Hank . . ." They shook. George and Shep also shook. Then Hank dropped his smoke, ground it out and pulled the roper's gloves from his belt-band and slowly put them on. "I got to pick up the B Bar horses and head on back," he said softly, avoiding the eyes of the other two. He did not move after he had the gloves on for a few moments. "I never did like good-byes," he said abruptly, and pushed on past to hasten inside the liverybarn. They heard him in there calling for the hostler to lead out those two B Bar critters George and Shep had ridden in last night.

Shep removed his hat, pushed a shirtsleeve across his face to wipe off perspiration, although it really wasn't very hot out back in the shade. Then he wagged his head. "That's a fact," he muttered, as though Hank were still there with them. "I never liked good-byes neither." He avoided looking at George for a moment, but when they heard someone inside the barn riding out the front way, Shep turned.

"With any luck me'n Billy Ray ought to be fifteen miles along by nightfall. George; care for a drink?"

George shook his head. "I kind of like the smell down here better too. Shep; good luck and a long life."

The raffish Texan smiled. "Same to you," he said, then turned away and also walked into the liverybarn.

George walked back up the rear alley as far as a vacant, weed-grown empty lot, then crossed through to the roadway and passed to the far side of the roadway, heading up towards the saloon. Abe Hepler, the bearded big blacksmith was emerging from the general store with a package and as they met Hepler smiled broadly. "I hear around town you're figurin' on opening up a harness shop across from my place," he said. "That's the best news I've heard in days. Shafter sure needs a feller like you, George. Even Herb Sloan agrees with that, and for Herb to say something is good, you know it's got to be plumb *awful* good."

George smiled. "Thanks," he said. "How's the lad?"

"My boy? Darned near well enough to band a fence-slat over his rear for what he done."

They laughed together and parted, Hepler hiking on across the road in the direction of his shop, George Lefton continuing on his way up to the Oxbow saloon.

The heat was rising steadily now, and as George reached the saloon overhang he saw a big dust-devil spiral to life a mile or so out across B Bar range where heat and wind combined to create this miniature kind of range-country twister. He stood watching, thinking that for the next few months there was going to be nothing but heat and drought, and of course all the complaining that went with both.

Natural calamities came, and they went. People survived. There really were no guarantees in this life; a man did what he thought he had to do, right or wrong, and none of it mattered a whole hell of a lot, because no man was ever here too long anyway, and afterwards there were still heat, and dust-devils, more calamities, and more people to carry on the tradition of survival.

He saw the rider coming from the south and turned. Shep trotted stiffly up the centre of the roadway. Their eyes met when they were abreast, and Shep gave that raffish smile and raised one gloved hand in a kind of laughing-sad salute. George offered the same kind of little acknowledgement, then Shep trotted on out of town to the north, and George waited until the Texan was lost to sight before he turned to enter the saloon and ask Dorry's brother how much rent he'd want for that empty store next to the emporium down the street.

The dust-devil died, the heat continued, the sun seemed not to be moving, and the first half of the life of a man — of *three* men in fact — had come and gone; had ended down there in the hot shade behind the old liverybarn.

Chapter Sixteen:
The Day to Remember

Herb Sloan was listening to a dusty rangerider over at his bar when George Lefton entered the saloon. There were three old men, and one empty chair, at a poker table over near the cold iron stove at the far north end of the room, playing cards beside a shaded window that offered a view of the yonder roadway. Otherwise the saloon was empty, which wasn't too surprising in mid-morning. As the heat mounted men would duck in and out all day long to get a glass of chilled beer, but they never tarried. The Oxbow would not start working towards a profit until evening, after supper and later.

George hardly more than glanced at the travel-stained cowboy as he ambled to the bar and bobbed his head at Herb, the usual signal for a glass of beer. Herb went to draw it off, and the dusty rider fished forth a silver coin, dropped it atop the bar, turned and walked out with his spurs tinkling.

Two blue-tailed flies, shiny and sleek as badgers, were making some kind of courting play upon the backbar shelf, and when Herb returned he hardly more than glanced at them before he upended a glass and caught them both very deftly beneath it.

Finding themselves imprisoned the flies exploded into frantic action and Herb put down George's beer as though he had done nothing unusual.

The flies were probably truants from the liverybarn anyway.

George tasted the beer, leaned down and said, "How much to rent that little store of yours down the road next to the general store?"

Herb's black eyes did not blink. "You got it," he said, around an unlighted cigar. "How much? Oh; maybe three dollars a month. That all right?"

George considered the unsmiling, beefy man, then drank a little more beer. "No, that's not all right," he said. "Dorry speak to you?"

Herb's eyes slithered away then back again. "Well; we talk a little now and then. She's my —"

"Don't beat around the bush with me, Herb."

Sloan's black eyes settled steadily upon George. "All right; we talked about your harness works down there. Any crime in that?"

George nodded. "Yeah. Dorry doesn't do my thinking for me. Neither do you."

Sloan bobbed his head. "All right. She

didn't mean any harm."

George was sure of that, so he finished the beer and smiled. "Let's start over. How much for that shop down the road?"

"Ten dollars a month. I had it rented to a feller last year for that."

George dug out a ten dollar note and put it upon the bar. "First month's rent," he said. "Herb, the next time Dorry gets helpful, tell her to stick to her knitting."

"Sure," muttered Sloan, scooping up the ten dollar note. He removed the cigar and closely examined the chewed end of it. "You got to understand something about my sister; she told me she likes you and she doesn't want you to ride on out." Herb plunged the cigar back into his mouth. He raised and lowered thick shoulders as though to imply none of this made a damned bit of sense to him. "I'm fond of her, so, when she does things, I usually want to help out."

George understood. He was fond of her too, and he would want to help out — but not as a brother, nor as a dominated lover or husband.

Herb finally lit the cigar. "Did you see that cowboy who was just in here?" he asked, and when George nodded Herb leaned atop his bar and dropped his voice. "He just rode over from the north range country. He run into a big drive over there heading west lookin' for free-graze. They told him they had a helluva fight with some fellers from over around Shafter, got their trailboss killed, got another feller with a busted arm, and had one rider quit and leave the country, all because they tried to bring their herd up onto the open range around Battle Mountain."

George said nothing. He and Herb Sloan exchanged a long look, then Herb picked up the empty glass and walked away to pump it full again, and return and set it down all without a word.

George drank a little of the beer. "Anything else?" he asked.

Herb frowned slightly. "No, I reckon not."

George considered; he knew perfectly well what Herb was wondering about. He also knew that as soon as B Bar reached town again, what had happened would no longer be a secret. "All right," he said. "That was my friends and me. Have you ever seen a real range war, Herb?"

"Yes, once, back in Missouri. Only it was more than just a range war."

"Messy?"

"Yes. And bloody, and pretty sickening."

"I've seen a couple of them too," stated

George. "So we rode over and turned those outsiders back. There wouldn't have been any fight if they hadn't tried stalking us to set up a bushwhack. The main thing is — no range war now."

Herb inclined his head. "All right." He smiled, a rare thing for Herb Sloan. Then he shoved out a pale thick hand. "Welcome to town, George."

Ten minutes later, fortified with two beers and the knowledge that he was now committed, George walked down the road southward with the key Herb Sloan had given him, and entered the empty store next to the emporium. It was cool inside, and it was also dingy with an accumulation of gloom that was at least in part the result of many years of heating the place in wintertime with a woodstove that had smoked up the ceiling and the walls.

He tilted back his hat, turned very slowly eyeing the sooty ceiling, and said aloud, "Paint."

From over near the alley doorway Dorry answered. "Lots of paint."

He looked at her as she moved from the deepest gloom. She handed him another key. "That's to the rear door." She smiled. "I saw you go into the Oxbow a little while ago, right after your friend rode out of town.

I guessed you'd talk to my brother about renting the store, so I came down the back way to be here and welcome you." Her liquid dark eyes brightened towards him. "A one-man welcoming committee."

He grinned back at her. "No, m'am; not even a blind person would ever mistake you for a one-*man* welcoming committee."

She blushed, but it was too gloomy for him to notice, then she went over where someone had nailed a newspaper picture of Ulysses S. Grant, many years back, and touched the wall. "The entire place has to be painted, George, walls, ceiling, woodwork." She turned. "Where would you put your work tables?"

He had only just walked into the building. "How would I know?" He twisted to look around. "One yonder against the wall, I reckon." He looked back. "I'm going to have to sort of feel my way along for a while, Dorry."

She started to say something, then slowly closed her mouth. For a while she watched him as he paced to the back-wall and turned to glance back towards the front window. "What did the last feller who rented this place use it for?"

She said, "He was going to start a newspaper, but when he went over to Deming to

172

see about buying a press, some newspaper over there hired him to replace an editor who had just died. That was a year or so ago. Since then my brother stored supplies for the saloon in here once in a while, otherwise it's been empty."

He shifted his attention from the sooty walls to her. She looked like a cameo-carving in this dismal setting, full and rounded and lovely, with a white dress forming a contrast to her black eyes and hair, and also to her golden face and throat and arms. Without moving from back near the end of the building he said, "Dorry . . . I paid Herb ten dollars. That's the rent from now on. Not three dollars. You understand?"

Evidently she understood, exactly, because she said, "Yes, George."

"And I won't need you to send those salesmen down to see me. I'll go over to Deming or maybe down to Lordburg, and get my supplies and tools and all."

"Yes, George."

"And . . ."

"Yes, George?"

He strolled forward, never taking his eyes off her. "Someday I've got something to tell you." He stopped directly in front of her, hooked his thumbs and wondered whether this might not be the time.

She scattered his thoughts with a sudden, quick question. "You're not married — somewhere?"

That startled him. "Married? Me? Lord no."

She loosened and the soft brilliance returned to her dark eyes. "Then I don't care what it is you'll tell me someday. George . . . I cooked a roast this afternoon."

He looked past her into the dazzling roadway. The last time he had noted the time, it had been morning.

She was right, though; now, it *was* afternoon.

"I also got a bottle of wine from Herb, if you'd like to have supper with me tonight, up at the dress shop."

His breath was beginning to come a little shallow, not just because of her although he never could have denied that she was principally the cause of how he felt right at this moment, but also because, of all the days in a man's life, there was usually one out of all the many days that he would never forget, one day that he *knew,* as surely as he knew he breathed, was the fateful day of his entire lifetime.

George had that unique knowledge now, as he stood with her. *This was that one day.*

He smiled. "What time do you want me

up there at the dress shop?"

"Six o'clock," she said, lilting the last of it almost as though it were a question.

He nodded. "I'll be there." He had more to say, but a man always has inhibitions. Any man has them.

She turned to walk towards the front door. He went along with her, and just before he reached past for the knob, she said, "George; that friend of yours — the big, smiling Texan . . . ?" She looked at him without completing her question.

"Gone," he told her. "When I was standing out front of the Oxbow, where you saw me, he was on his way then."

She proved herself a perceptive woman. "I know. I watched. I saw how he looked at you and how you waved back."

He opened the door. "Six o'clock, Dorry."

She smiled, walked past out upon the shaded plank-walk, and beyond her out in the roadway the doctor's dusty old worn topbuggy went ploddingly past. The doctor raised an arm. George waved, then Dorry turned and also waved.

After she left, George went back into the shop and stood a while before he locked up, front and back, and went over to the tonsorial parlour to get the key to the bathhouse.

He had several hours, so he was in no

hurry. He bought new trousers and a new blue shirt at the general store. He got some harness wax from the liveryman and worked hard to make his boots presentable. Then he went over to get shaved and to take his bath. A man always felt different after a bath, especially in summertime.

Herb was out front of the saloon talking to a burly, shaggy-headed freighter when George came along. Herb introduced them, then said to the freighter that George was going to open a harness shop in Shafter. The shaggy-headed freighter's eyes brightened with sharp interest. "Mister," he boomed, "that's the best news I ever got out of this tarnal town. When'll you be ready for business? I got a whole shedfull of tore collars, busted britchings, old traces and whatnots up north, and there ain't a place I can get 'em fixed proper between Raton and Lordsburg."

George laughed. "Give me two weeks to get set up," he said, and pumped the powerful hand of the freighter, then went inside the saloon.

Herb got behind his bar, then wrinkled his nose. "You been to the barber?"

George looked over. "Why; does it smell that bad?"

Herb filled two small, delicate glasses with

white wine, something George had never seen him do before in the Oxbow. He pushed one forward as he said, "Well; it's a different smell than I'm used to when rangemen come in." He lifted the delicate glass. "To your success . . . and to anything else you figure needs a blessing and a toast." Herb knew; George could read it in his face. How *much* he knew was something George would never fathom, but Herb was also a man.

They drank, then, as Herb put the little glass down gently he jerked a thick thumb over his shoulder. "You can have that painting of Dorry."

George looked upwards. "You know, when I first saw that, I didn't think it was of a real woman."

Herb turned and scowled upwards. "Feller that painted that, back in Missouri, got drowned six months later trying to float a wagon across the river to come west. He . . . well; it doesn't matter anyway. He's dead now. Been dead some time in fact; quite a few years."

George dropped his gaze to Herb's face. "He was in love with her?"

Herb nodded. "But you see, when he painted that, she was just fresh out of pigtails."

George leaned, gazing upwards again. "She hasn't changed though, Herb."

Sloan sighed. "I sure hope to hell she has. Well; she is a woman now."

George nodded. There was no point in him confirming this.

"I'll take the picture down tomorrow," Herb said, and avoided George's eyes as he cleared his throat. Obviously, Dorry and her brother had had more than just a *little* talk.

George asked what time it was. Herb dug out his big gold watch, flipped open the hunting case, looked, then closed the case and returned the watch to his pocket. "The sun doesn't go down as soon as it did a few months back," he said. "Hard to tell just by looking at it, isn't it?"

"What time is it?" reiterated George.

"Half past five."

George reached in a pocket to pay for the wine but Herb shook his head. "I never charge for that, and I only pour it on special occasions."

George smiled. "Thank you. See you tomorrow."

Herb leaned as he said, "Yeah," very softly, and watched George Lefton walk out of his saloon.

Chapter Seventeen:
Dorry Sloan — And Sunset

Dorry's quarters behind her dress shop were surprisingly large and comfortable. George had had some idea there would be perhaps two or three small rooms. There were five rooms and none of them were small.

She didn't light the lamps because the sun was still up when he arrived, and she took him on through where the parlour was. Beyond it was the dining-room, and beyond that was the kitchen where all the wonderful aromas came from. She went to get him a glass of wine, and when she returned he eyed the clear liquid thoughtfully; it was the same kind of wine her brother had just served him not fifteen minutes earlier. Maybe Herb had been trying to convey something.

Dorry had her black hair piled high. She had changed from the white dress to a sleeveless light tan blouse, probably because it was hot even with all the windows open. Her arms were strong and firm and golden. George sipped his wine and watched her leave the room to check something in the kitchen, and when she returned he watched her again.

Charley Santee had never said a truer thing in his life; she *was* the most beautiful woman George had ever seen. She wanted to refill his glass, and leaned to do it. She was a high-breasted, sturdy woman. George watched the wine bubble into his glass, watched the pulse in the V of her throat, and when she straightened up again, he put the glass aside and arose.

She met his quiet glance without flinching. For five seconds neither of them moved, then Dorry turned, set the bottle aside and straightened up again. He reached, and she came into his arms without any hesitation. Her arms came up and closed over his shoulders.

For a while he held her without moving. He had to speak, but the words eluded him. Evidently her poise was better because she said, "Will you promise me something?"

He bobbed his head with the clean scent of her hair in his face. "Sure."

"You won't leave Shafter?"

He pulled back and looked down into her lifted face. "If I leave Shafter, Dorry, you'll have to come with me."

She stood up to her full height against him. He lowered his head, and when their lips met he felt a sudden, totally soundless explosion deep inside. His arms tightened.

Her hands flattened with hard pressure, and when she responded to his fire with a surge of fierce need and hunger, he had to loosen his grip a little.

He felt like a man who had been holding his breath under water; it was like surfacing at the very last minute, but he controlled his breathing with a powerful effort. She smiled upwards, not the least bit abashed. "I've got to go finish setting the table," she said quietly, but did not release him. "You can help, if you'd like to."

He did not let her go. "In a moment, Dorry."

She continued to look up at him. He could not meet her gaze for a moment or two, not until her breathing was less tremulous, then he stepped away, caught her hands as he brought her arms down, and said, "Will you marry me, Dorry?"

She did not hesitate this time either. "Yes."

He did not know what to say next, but again she saved him. She swung his arms wide and stepped in close again, buried her face against his chest and clung to him.

Outside, some riders loped past, entering town from either the north or the east, and one of them called out something cheerfully to the others, the sounds faded, and no doubt those cowboys had turned in farther

181

along at the Oxbow hitchrail.

The sun was teetering upon a faraway bony ridge, shadows crept stealthily from around the buildings on the west side of town, and over where that ancient corral stood, broken now beyond use or repair, where George had first spoken to Dorry Sloan, a couple of mongrel dogs went stiff-stepping around each other, hackles up, not quite willing to fight yet, but toying with the idea.

She turned, finally, and pulled him along with her to the dining-room. He thought the table looked very handsome; there were two heavy silver candlesticks, which she told him later had belonged to her mother, and there were dishes and glassware and even a linen tablecloth. He wondered what more had to be put upon the table.

She showed him. Bread and butter and some kind of sauce, which was like gravy, she had made to go with their roast beef.

He was beginning to acquire his education as a domesticated man then and there. He liked it. Mainly because every time he looked around, she was there doing something, and no matter how he saw her, head-on, liquid dark eyes softly on him, or profiled — sturdy and strong and golden in the fading daylight — his breath hung up just a little. Charley Santee had been *so awfully* right.

She went after his abandoned wine glass and when he accepted it from her he leaned and kissed her cheek. She stood perfectly motionless until he drew back a little, then she looked tenderly at him.

"George, there is something you're suppose to say to a woman before you ask her to marry you."

He thought a moment. "Oh." He felt the heat in his face. "I love you, Dorry."

She slid her arms round his middle, almost upsetting the wine in his hand, and squeezed with surprising strength, then she suddenly let go, turned her back on him and went quickly back into the kitchen.

We hope you have enjoyed this Large Print book. Other Thorndike, Wheeler, and Chivers Press Large Print books are available at your library or directly from the publishers.

For information about current and upcoming titles, please call or write, without obligation, to:

Publisher
Thorndike Press
295 Kennedy Memorial Drive
Waterville, ME 04901
Tel. (800) 223-1244

or visit our Web site at:

www.gale.com/thorndike
www.gale.com/wheeler

OR

Chivers Large Print
published by BBC Audiobooks Ltd
St James House, The Square
Lower Bristol Road
Bath BA2 3SB
England
Tel. +44(0) 800 136919
email: bbcaudiobooks@bbc.co.uk
www.bbcaudiobooks.co.uk

All our Large Print titles are designed for easy reading, and all our books are made to last.